He was obviously hungry

Elena couldn't have looked away from Matt's devouring gaze if she'd tried. The room was suddenly warm, surrounding them like a cocoon.

Anticipation surged through her as Matt slowly put down his fork and stood. When he reached out to her, she rose willingly to be enfolded in his strong embrace. Eagerly she returned his deep kisses.

When he finally raised his head and spoke, the desire in his voice mirrored his own longing. "Let's leave this, shall we?" He nodded toward the table.

Elena smiled provocatively and ran her hand over his chest. "But dessert..."

His arms still holding her to him, he began walking toward the stairs. "Let's make it together...."

Janice Kay Johnson lives just north of Seattle with her husband and two children (one of them brand-new!). A former librarian, Janice began writing romances in collaboration with her mother under the name Kay Kirby. Solo, she went on to write as Janice Stevens.

Night and Day is her first Harlequin Temptation. The inspiration for this charming story came out of Jan's own interest in pottery.

Books by Janice Kay Johnson

HARLEQUIN REGENCY ROMANCE
13—THE IMPERILED HEIRESS

Night and Day

JANICE KAY JOHNSON

Harlequin Books

TORONTO • NEW YORK • LONDON
AMSTERDAM • PARIS • SYDNEY • HAMBURG
STOCKHOLM • ATHENS • TOKYO • MILAN

Published April 1987

ISBN 0-373-25249-8

1

ELENA WAS over an hour late for her appointment, and the bank would be closing any minute. Still, she hesitated before shutting off her car's engine. She knew the old Volkswagen wouldn't start again. At home she'd given it a running start, then the car had stalled at a deserted intersection with no convenient hill in sight. She had been forced to wait until a sympathetic motorist had stopped to give her a push start.

Now when she turned the key off, the engine backfired and the car shook for a second before falling silent. Elena gave the plastic steering wheel a gentle farewell pat before picking up her handbag and climbing out.

MATT TERRELL'S undivided attention should have been devoted to the papers spread across his desk. A decision had to be made soon, and with the future of interest rates as uncertain as it was, the answer was far from straightforward. He'd been nagged by just a hint of spring fever all day, however. Through the glass walls of his office he could see across the foyer to the front door, which offered a tantalizing glimpse of green grass and golden sunlight.

He glanced up yet again when that door swung open, but his unfocused gaze sharpened the moment he saw the woman was entering. It was her long, slender legs that first caught his attention, and then her hair, a thick mass of shimmering honey caught back in a loose chignon. He imagined with pleasure how it would look in the sunlight, rich in color. He liked, too, her air of natural elegance, epitomized by the easy, unself-conscious way she moved. Her clothes, an off-white linen suit and chocolate silk blouse, were understated but striking. Matt found himself wondering what color her eyes were and how she would look when she smiled. Not, he thought with a sigh, that he was ever likely to know. His job description didn't include waylaying clients for such unbusinesslike reasons. And unfortunately, she was heading toward the tellers' cages, not his office.

ELENA COULD TELL as she walked across the plush green carpet toward the teller's window that the bank's activity was winding down for the day. Almost all of the desks were deserted. Probably she was too late. And a banker wouldn't appreciate a client who missed an appointment without giving him notice. Although, since she was here for a car loan, she thought she had merely proven the urgency of her need.

The teller, a dark-haired young woman, looked up with a smile. "Can I help you?"

"I'm not sure. I had an appointment with Mr. Glover for three-thirty. I'm afraid I had car trouble, and as you can see I'm very late. Is there any chance . . . ?" She paused hopefully.

The teller was shaking her head. "Mr. Glover has gone for the day. He did mention that someone had failed to keep an appointment." Her expression now held faint condemnation, although her tone was still pleasant. "I suggest you reschedule. Perhaps you could call tomorrow?"

Elena almost groaned. With her most persuasive smile she said, "It's very difficult for me to get here." That, she thought, picturing her dead car in the bank lot, was the understatement of the year. "Is there any possibility that someone else could see me?"

Again the teller shook her head. "The other loan officers are gone, also. It's very late. We're about ready to close."

Elena let out a long, defeated breath. "Thank you," she said mechanically, and had begun to turn away when a deep voice intervened.

"What seems to be the problem?"

A man had come out of the glass-fronted office to the left of the tellers' cages and was walking soundlessly across the thick carpet toward Elena. His presence dominated the room, although his coloring and dress were the opposite of flamboyant. He was tall, with broad, muscular shoulders and the relaxed, unconscious grace of an athlete. He had a thin, tanned face with an angular jaw and a narrow, patrician nose. He was handsome, but not remarkably so. His pale blond hair was cut conventionally short, and he wore a well-tailored gray suit and crisp white shirt. The qualities that made his presence so potent were more indefinable: the way he held his head, the silver-gray eyes, the straight line of his mouth, which gave the impression of carefully concealed emotions.

His gaze took in Elena's slender length and flicked back to her face, but polite inquiry was all she read in his eyes. A surprising stab of disappointment at his lack of open reaction to her as a woman held Elena, for a rare moment, speechless.

The teller's babble indicated that she was no more immune to his magnetism than was Elena. "Oh, Mr. Terrell, this lady was late for an appointment. Mr. Glover has already gone for the day. I suggested she re-schedule. I'm sure there'll be no problem—"

He smoothly cut her off. "And what was the appointment about?"

Elena found her tongue. "A car loan," she said quickly. "And I'm desperate."

Amused by her willingness to seize the opportunity, Matt smiled. "We don't want to turn away a client in distress," he said, inclining his head toward the open office door. "This way."

The glass door had discreet gold letters on it that announced, M. Terrell, V.P. Matt saw the interested glance Elena gave it, and wondered if she was as curious to know his first name as he was to know hers. He hoped so. The instant attraction he had felt when she'd walked in the door had only been compounded by a closer look. Her features were classic: high cheekbones and forehead, a slender nose and delicate chin. And when her gaze had turned to him, the wide gray eyes were direct and intelligent.

Matt didn't recall ever being pleased before when a client had a problem that required his intervention so close to closing time, but when he'd seen the disappointment on her face as she had begun to turn away, he had found himself on his feet and heading toward her. He didn't regret his impulse now, even though the day had been a long one that she would make longer.

After politely pulling a chair forward for her, he sat behind the modern oak desk. "I'm Matt Terrell," he said.

"Elena Simpson," she returned pleasantly. She reminded herself that no matter how much she was attracted to him physically and warmed by the ready humor his smile had displayed, it would be foolish to forget that he was a businessman. And a bank vice president was bound to care more for dollars and cents than for people. She reached in her purse and pulled out a white envelope. "Here's my completed loan application."

"Fine. That saves time." He withdrew the form from the envelope and bent his head to study it.

Elena looked at the strong brown fingers that held the paper and wondered how he had acquired such a dark tan. It was only just May, and in the state of Washington even skiers weren't that dark, especially after an unusually drippy spring. She pulled together the tatters of cynicism she reserved for men such as him and decided he probably used a tanning salon.

"Occupation: potter?" He looked from the paper to her face.

"Yes," she answered with composure. "I make pots. Stoneware."

"Mmm." His gaze sharpened, and she felt as though a spotlight was trained on her. "Do you work for someone, or are you self-employed?"

She didn't point out that his question had been answered in her neatest printing on the application. After all, it was late, and she was grateful to him for seeing her. What's more, experience told her that this was the critical moment in the interview; her status as a loan prospect was bound to decline when he found out she didn't receive a regular paycheck.

"Self-employed."

"Do you have . . . um, what are they called? Kiln openings?"

"That *is* what they're called," she supplied, surprised at his knowledge, "but, no, I don't have them. I work at home, and it's too isolated. I sell at shows and to several shops in the area."

"You mention an income figure here," he said. "Is it—" he searched for a tactful choice of words "—variable?"

Elena hesitated, then finally conceded, "Yes, of course it is to a degree. Sometimes I do make less, but then sometimes I make more. I wouldn't have applied for the loan if my income weren't steady enough to make the payments." She waited anxiously for his response. If this bank where she kept her accounts wouldn't give her the loan, would any other?

"I'm sure that's true," he agreed politely, but his mouth had a skeptical twist that reminded her he must daily see people who didn't fulfill their obligations. He went on, "You're not planning to buy a new car?"

"That I can't afford," she said frankly, "Besides, to be honest, I don't much care about cars. I just want something to get me around."

"And your present one doesn't?"

"No. It's the reason I was late for my appointment." She paused, wondering how much to tell him, then gave a shrug. "Actually, it won't start anymore, among other problems. At home I have a slope to get it going on, but on the way here I stalled at a stop sign and had to wait until someone gave me a jump start."

Astonishingly, his eyes narrowed with definite amusement. "This bank is on very flat land. Nary a hill around."

Elena was surprised at his quickness and apparent sense of humor. Her ancient Volkswagen would look a bit incongruous as a permanent fixture in the bank's parking lot. Trying to keep a straight face, she said, "I noticed."

"Are you offering it to us as collateral?" he asked.

"Something like that," she agreed, chuckling. "Actually, I planned to have it towed away. I'm buying a Volkswagen bus from Import Motors down the road, and they knocked a hundred dollars off the price in exchange for old Bessie out there. They're going to use her for parts."

He frowned. "Isn't a bus a peculiar choice for a woman?"

Her expression cooled. "It being difficult for the delicate little woman to drive?"

"You can lower your chin," he said amiably, unoffended. "Getting one of those beasts in reverse practically takes a black belt in karate, you know."

She let her features relax. "Yes, I know," she admitted, "but it's perfect for hauling pottery around. Not to mention dogs."

"Dogs?" His tone was incredulous, and his gaze traveled slowly from the smooth sweep of her hair to the silk bow at her neck and the crisp linen jacket.

She tried to ignore the prickling down her spine that his appraisal produced. "I have two golden retrievers. They didn't fit very well in my bug," she said calmly.

"I can imagine." He smiled faintly and shook his head, then went back to reading her application with even more interest than before, wondering what other surprises he would find. If he'd had to peg her on sight, he would have guessed she was a professional woman— a lawyer, perhaps, or a manager. It intrigued him to discover how far off he'd been and made him want to know more about her.

As he read Elena studied the top of his head, wondering why he didn't let his hair grow longer. It looked as though it would be silky and soft to the touch, and she could imagine running her hand through it. She stamped on the thought as quickly as it had come to her.

After a moment Matt looked up, pretending he wasn't aware of her scrutiny. "I don't see any problem. You're not asking for much, and it looks like you should be able to handle the payments all right. We'll have to do a credit check before this is okayed, though."

"Yes, of course. Will it take long?"

"A few days. You really are desperate, aren't you?" She nodded. "I'm carless."

"So I gathered." He stood and dropped her application in a wire basket on the corner of the desk without looking away from her face. "Is someone picking you up?"

She hesitated. "I intended to call a friend."

Once again surrendering to impulse, Matt offered casually, "I'd be happy to give you a lift home." For once he was ready to dismiss from his mind the work left undone on his desk; it would still be there tomorrow.

He could see that Elena was taken aback by his suggestion, and a hint of a frown creased her forehead. "Thank you," she said, standing. "It's kind of you to offer, but I think I should make other arrangements."

Matt was uncomfortably aware of their situation, which placed her in an undeniably awkward position. This wasn't quite as bad as a doctor asking his patient for a date, but it was far from ideal. She'd come to him for business reasons, and until the loan was approved he held the upper hand. What he should do was make a note of her telephone number, which was on her application, wait a polite two weeks and then call her. That way, if she wanted to turn him down she could do so without feeling pressured.

On the other hand, it didn't seem to him that her refusal had been quite as firm as it might have been. Perhaps she really was stuck for a ride home but didn't want his charity.

He made one more try, his tone undemanding. "It wouldn't be any trouble," he said. "I'm in no hurry to get anywhere tonight."

She hesitated again, wondering about his motives, then said weakly, "I live out in the boonies. It's a thirty-five minute drive from Snohomish."

Not by a flicker of an eyelash did Matt reveal his satisfaction. "That's fine," he said. "I enjoy seeing a little of the countryside."

Elena felt guiltily that she was taking advantage of his courtesy, but the idea of being driven to her doorstep was too seductive. She smiled gratefully and said, "In that case, thank you."

He simply nodded, his expression matter-of-fact, and held open the office door for her. He gave some instructions to his secretary that made Elena realize that on her account he was leaving work rather earlier than he had intended. A moment later they were out in the afternoon sunlight.

Matt nodded toward the faded red Volkswagen she had parked as inconspicuously as possible in the far corner of the lot. "Yours?" he inquired. "Would you like to stop at the garage and ask them to tow it?"

She laughed. "Do I detect some ulterior motive here? Don't you think old Bessie enhances your bank's image?"

"She may make it seem a little homier," he agreed, not responding to her accusation. She concluded that he was indeed anxious to see the last of her decrepit car.

"If you don't mind stopping," she said, "I'd appreciate it. It'll save me a long distance call. I'm always watching my pennies, Mister Banker."

Elena wasn't surprised when he stopped at a charcoal gray Mercedes sedan. She could see why he hadn't offered to give her a push start, and as he unlocked the car, she looked at the shiny paint job with misgivings. The last several miles of her road were not only rutted after the winter and filled with potholes, they were overgrown with blackberry and alder. She always drove with her car windows rolled up because of the way the branches scratched and whipped at her car.

"Mr. Terrell," she began.

"Matt," he corrected.

"Matt. I think maybe it would be better if I called one of my friends to pick me up." Suddenly realizing how that sounded, she hastily explained, "The road I live on is a mess. I don't want to see you get a scratch on your car or get stuck."

"Don't be ridiculous. Mercedes aren't built to be delicate." He opened the passenger-side door and, with a gentle pressure of his hand on her elbow, urged her forward.

She capitulated and settled into the soft black leather upholstery. The situation seemed so unlikely she had a sensation of being swept away, kidnapped. There were worse ways to go, though, she decided, as Matt turned the key in the ignition and the engine started with a purr instead of the coughs, wheezes and rattles to which she was accustomed. As the car moved out of the parking lot and into the street, Elena couldn't even feel the bumps. It moved with a powerful, relaxed grace, as its master did, she thought, casting a sidelong glance at Matt Terrell.

He stopped the car at the garage, and Elena went in to make arrangements with Jerry, the owner. When she got back into the Mercedes, she spoke without looking at Matt. "Thanks for stopping. He's going to go get Bessie this evening."

Matt was half turned toward her, and his arm was stretched along the back of her seat. Elena felt self-conscious settling back, aware as she was of his hand only inches from the coil of hair at her nape. After a quiet moment, during which Matt didn't move to start the car, Elena directed an inquiring look at him.

Matt was waging an internal battle. He wanted very much to spend more time with Elena, to have a chance to move their relationship to some other footing than a banker doing his client a favor. Specifically, he wanted to have dinner with her. Unfortunately, the same objection that had occurred to him in his office still stood, only with an addition. Now she depended on him for a ride as well as for the loan. He told himself, without much resolve, that it wasn't fair to put her on the spot. If only he knew that she'd shared the instant rush of physical attraction he had felt!

Suddenly he realized that the silence had stretched on far too long and that Elena's gray eyes held puzzlement. She probably thought he regretted his offer of a ride home and was simply hesitating over telling her so.

Her words confirmed his suspicion. "I was just thinking," she said. "Maybe it would be best if I rent a loaner from Jerry here. Then I wouldn't have to inconvenience you—"

Matt held up his left hand to stop her. "It's not an inconvenience," he assured her. "In fact, to the contrary. I was just wondering how to ask you to have dinner with me without making you feel pressured. I'd very much like you to, but if you'd rather not I'll be happy to take you straight home."

Elena was dumbfounded. Was that the tiniest trace of uncertainty, anxiety that she saw in his face? She felt unreasonably flattered by his invitation, and the first stirrings of excitement quivered in her stomach. She knew she should refuse, that she was unlikely to have much in common with a confident young banker, but the physical pull she felt was stronger.

Before she could change her mind she said firmly, "Thank you, I'd like to have dinner with you."

"Good." The direct look he gave her before his heavy gold lashes shaded his eyes quickened the excitement within her from a trickle to a tide. Still without touching her, he removed his arm from the seat and reached for the ignition. "Is Terrenzio's all right?" he asked.

"I love it." She found his suggestion unexpected; although the food was fantastic at Terrenzio's, the restaurant was small and the decor simple. Somehow, she pictured Matt Terrell as more the white tablecloth and candlelight type. She was glad she was going to have the chance to find out what he was really like.

2

THE RESTAURANT was only about a mile down the road from the garage. The floor was paved with red tiles, and the walls were white plaster, decorated with bright posters depicting scenes of Italy. The small wood tables and bentwood chairs were crowded into the narrow room; at peak hours the diners were practically elbow to elbow.

They were led by a teenage waitress to a tiny table by the lace-curtained window. The table had a wine bottle in the center, with one red rose sticking out of it. After some consultation, Matt ordered the cannelloni and Elena the fettuccine Alfredo.

"Shall we just have the house wine?" Matt asked, and she nodded.

Matt leaned back, resting one elbow on the windowsill. His legs were stretched out under the table, and Elena turned a little sideways so her feet didn't touch his. She wished the tables weren't so small, and he wasn't so close. His expression was no longer reserved, and he seemed to be shedding his formality. For the first time Elena could imagine him clothed in something other than a suit. As he shifted in his chair the fabric of his coat stretched taut across the long muscles of his upper arm.

"Tell me about your potting," he said after a moment. "You said you work at home."

Elena was glad to talk of something so familiar, although she suspected any tension was in her own mind. She told him that she had a potting wheel in a sun porch attached to the side of her house, but that her kiln and storage shelves were in a shed. "It's sort of inconvenient," she admitted ruefully, "but this way I can work in a room that's heated in the winter. I can't afford to renovate the shed and insulate it. Of course the finished pots don't care. Someday I'd like a better setup, but . . ." She shrugged.

"What kind of things do you make?" he asked. His gaze was disturbingly intent.

"Dishes and plant pots. I don't make purely decorative items or sculpture," she explained. "The plant pots are the most easily salable, but there's a good market for casseroles and serving dishes. I make sets of plates and bowls, and of course mugs. I also do some custom work; the buyer tells me what color and shape he wants, and voilà—I produce."

She was a little surprised to see he looked genuinely interested, then realized with some embarrassment that she wasn't at all sure she wanted to hear, in turn, about his work. She thought banks and money were boring. Believing it to be the practical option, she'd majored in business in college and found all of the course work to be hideously dull.

"Do you ever get bored?" he asked, uncannily echoing her thoughts. Almost at once he smiled apologetically. "It's not that potting sounds uninteresting, but . . .

Oh, I'd think after a while one mug would start to look just like the last."

"And dollar bills don't?" she inquired politely.

He grinned. "Touché! Although actually, mere dollars exist to bore my tellers. Paperwork is my nemesis. Do you have any idea how often I sign my name every day? I like to think I'd notice if I were putting my John Henry on something with too many zeros, but I'm not positive. I may make one of my employees very rich someday."

Elena chuckled. "You'd better whisper when you say that. You might give somebody ideas!"

"Heaven forbid! But now that I've confessed, it's your turn. Do you get bored?"

She answered truthfully, "I try hard not to let that happen. I'm always experimenting with new shapes. And the glazes are always different. When you think about it, there's an endless range of new colors and forms. Naturally I'm always trying to get better at what I do. Besides, to me the wheel work is tremendously relaxing." Without understanding why, she found she badly wanted to convey her experience to him. She held out her hands, cupping them as though they were cradling a ball of soft clay, and said, "The clay has this texture—either slippery smooth or rough, depending on what type I'm using—and it changes shape almost magically as I touch it. The wheel is going around and around. That centers my attention. When I'm throwing a pot I don't usually think about anything else." She smiled and leaned back in her chair. "I'm not as fond of some of the other jobs. I have to force myself to foot the pots, and I don't like loading the kiln very well, although unloading it is great! I see how everything came out."

As he listened Matt was warmed by her enthusiasm and even more by her apparent eagerness to share it with him. The work he did offered satisfaction of the mind and not the senses. Matt had never known an artisan well before and had no such leanings himself, but Elena had brought vividly alive the tactual and sensory pleasure her art gave her; he could feel it and in doing so learned something important about her.

"Back to the subject of being bored," she added, before he had a chance to comment, "I have to admit I don't work full-time. I think anything done eight hours a day would become boring. I raise some of my own food, and that takes time, and I just read, and . . . Well, to be honest, I don't try to discipline myself too much."

Without thinking, Matt said dryly, "Nice for you. Everybody would like to do that, but most of us have to make a living." He realized immediately how critical he had sounded and grinned ruefully. "Oops. That sounded stuffy, didn't it?"

Although Elena acknowledged his chagrin with a faint smile, her eyes were cool. "I know better than to comment on that," she said lightly. "But in answer to what you said, well, I have to make a living, too. I simply don't see any purpose in turning my life into a rat race and losing the quality time just to make lots of money that I don't really need. It's remarkable how little I need. I think most people would find they're the same, if they just took a good look at their life-styles."

"Meaning me?" he asked with interest.

"Not at all." Feeling unexpectedly flustered, Elena took refuge in a slow sip of wine. Crossing her legs, she smoothed down her skirt. "I don't know anything about your life-style, so I can hardly comment, can I?"

She thought it wouldn't be hard to make some rather accurate guesses. That made her wonder why she had allowed herself to be persuaded—and so easily—to have dinner with Matt Terrell. He could have come straight from the pages of *Esquire*, while she, when in her usual guise, fit *Mother Earth News*. And, although there was no physical resemblance, he suddenly reminded her rather too much of her father, who was a successful stockbroker. It would be wise, she thought, to keep that resemblance in mind. With this man it was undoubtedly safer to have some defenses.

Their food arrived just then, and the conversation was allowed to drop. After a few bites, Matt asked, "Do you like to travel? Or is that one of the sacrifices you have to make for quality time?"

The humor in his voice robbed this remark of any edge, and she was able to respond equably, "Yes, I do enjoy traveling. I've been wondering where you got such a nice tan." She hoped she'd put him on the spot, so that he would have to confess to frequenting a tanning salon.

Instead he said, "I just spent a couple of weeks in Mexico."

"Acapulco?" she asked. "Puerto Vallarta?"

His brows rose in amusement, and he said, "I think you have me stereotyped!"

Elena flushed a deep red. She mumbled, "I'm sorry. I just . . . That's where most people go."

"Actually I was on the Yucatán Peninsula," he said, taking pity on her. "Went to Chichén Itzá, some of the other ruins. I'm interested in archeology."

"Are you?" Elena's discomfiture of a moment before vanished, and she said eagerly, "I am, too. I envy you. That sounds like a wonderful trip. One of my dreams is to go to South America, and see Machu Picchu."

"I've been," he admitted. "I'd like to go back, though. The weather was poor when I was there, and while a damp mist does provide a certain atmosphere, it doesn't do much for the view. Or for taking pictures, which is another of my hobbies. I could have bought some, of course, but it's just not the same."

She agreed. "Postcards never look like the same place you've been, do they? I just use an Instamatic, though, so my photo album isn't anything to brag about."

They talked about traveling in Europe, then, as they'd both been. Elena had actually spent two summers wandering through Europe, the first, with her parents, when she was sixteen staying in nice hotels. The second time, between her junior and senior years in college, she'd had a Eurail pass and all her belongings had been on her back. Matt confessed to having gone the Hilton route, but he seemed fascinated by her stories of hitching rides and scrounging places to sleep.

"I can't say I envy you not being able to find a washing machine for two weeks," he commented at last, "but it does sound like you met interesting people."

Elena tried to ignore the unspoken and possibly imagined, "better you than me." "I thought so," she said evenly. Then she deliberately changed the subject. "Tell me, did you make it to Athens?"

It turned out that they had been to many of the same places, and fond reminiscences took them enjoyably through dinner.

Matt was just saying, "The Parthenon was ruined for me by the mobs and by those damn guards running around blowing their whistles. It looked and sounded like a crowded gymnasium," when the bill arrived. He reached for his wallet and, with one of those smiles that softened his face to a remarkable degree said, "I guess I should prepare myself for the great journey to your place, shouldn't I?"

Elena had to laugh. "It's not that bad! It is a little convoluted, though, so you'd better pay attention or you might not make it back."

It had become dark while they ate, and Elena could feel a difference in the atmosphere as soon as they got back into the car. The subtly lit restaurant, the other diners and the relaxed conversation had begun to make her feel comfortable; she'd lost some of that prickly awareness of his physical presence. Now the darkness pressed at the car windows, making the interior a small, warm oasis from the night, and the passing lights seemed very far away and unreal. Somehow the front seat of the car seemed smaller than it had before. Trying not to be obvious, Elena sat as far from Matt as she could, although she remained all to conscious of his thigh just on the other side of the console and the bulk of his shoulders.

Just when the silence had begun to seem unnatural, Matt asked, "How did you come to live so far out?"

"Actually," she admitted, "it started as one of my father's brainstorms. He thought everyone should invest in real estate as soon as they could possibly afford it—although now that I think about it, that's an odd notion for a stockbroker. When I got my first job out of college he helped me buy ten acres out here. It's so isolated the price was low, and of course my father never dreamed I'd actually live here. Originally I was just supposed to be buying on spec."

"And so why did you end up here?"

Unwilling to take a chance on being mocked, Elena shrugged. "Why not?"

There was a little silence, during which Matt contemplated the wound he'd apparently probed inadvertently. Finally he said, "I take it your father doesn't approve?"

"You take it right." Elena sighed. "We have a running battle, or at least we did. I think maybe he's given up. He lives in San Francisco, so I just get letters from my mother saying, 'Your father suggests . . .'"

"Which you duly throw in the trash can."

"Not at all," Elena said lightly. "I answer them, like a good daughter should. And I send them pots for their birthdays and Christmas."

He laughed at the picture she was painting. "Which your mother never uses, as she undoubtedly sets her table with Lennox and Waterford."

"Actually, she claims to like my casseroles. She tells all her friends I made them, and they tell her what a creative daughter she has."

"Do I detect a note of bitterness?"

She sighed again. "No, I don't think so. At least, I hope not. I'm fairly close to my mother, and she tries not to make judgments about my life-style. I just sometimes wish . . ." She stared ahead into the darkness, momentarily forgetting her companion's existence. "I wish her values were different so she could be proud of me, not just pretend to be."

When he made no comment, she sneaked a glance at Matt's shadowed face, wondering what expression it held. She didn't understand what had driven her to put into words her troubled relationship with her parents; she seldom thought about it, and made a point of not discussing it, even with friends. She supposed it was just the darkness that made it easy to talk, and the unexpected empathy she had sensed from this man.

Matt wasn't certain how to respond. He hadn't missed that last glance, which made him wonder if Elena hadn't told him more about herself than she'd intended. He guessed she had a strong desire for privacy—despite the relaxed warmth that so attracted him—and that now wasn't the moment to probe. There would be another time, when she knew him and had more reason to trust him.

"Are you safe out here?" he asked. "Don't you worry about being so isolated?"

Elena produced her stock answer. "I'm safer here than I would be in the city. I do have neighbors, you know. And, by the way, my turn is right up here."

He eased the car onto the narrow gravel road. They passed several lighted houses before she had him turn again into a still narrower lane. Trailing brambles snapped against the windshield, and despite the superior suspension of the Mercedes, its passengers were jarred by the occasional unavoidable pothole. Once, when the left wheel dropped into a deep rut, Elena was thrown sideways against Matt's shoulder. With a mumbled apology she pulled herself upright, glad the darkness hid her consternation. It was absurd to be so self-conscious about such physical contact. With any of her friends she would either have been unaware of briefly colliding or laughed it off.

The car bounced again, and Matt exclaimed, "Can't you do anything about this road?" He wondered incredulously, how could she endure this day in and day out?

Elena's hands tightened in her lap. "What am I supposed to do?"

"Get the county to fix it, what else?"

"It's not a county road, or... At least, I guess it is, but most of this land isn't developed yet, so they don't want to waste money maintaining it. And I can't afford to. I wish I could, because of my work. I have to swaddle every piece of pottery like it's a baby before I box it, and I have old quilts in the car I set the boxes on to cushion the ride. But as long as I can get in and out..."

"It's no wonder your Volkswagen is shot."

Elena bit her lower lip and refrained from a retort. She had suddenly remembered that, as well as being the man who had taken her to dinner, he was also the banker who had yet to approve her car loan.

In a small voice, she said, "That's my drive on the right." When the car stopped in front of the wood gate, she hurriedly climbed out to open it, before he could chivalrously insist on doing so. When the car came abreast of her, she slid back in, leaving the gate open for his departure.

The driveway wound for several hundred yards through a thick stand of evergreens, then abruptly emerged into a clearing. As always, when she planned to be gone for several hours, she had left on the porch light and a floodlight attached to the shed. Illuminated this way, her small log house looked like a miniature fortress, built to withstand the assaults of hostile tribes.

Matt stopped the car in front of the shed and switched off the engine. In the sudden silence he looked around. They both heard the howling at the same time; it was coming from the woods and steadily growing in volume.

He directed a look of amused astonishment at her and said, "Wolves?"

She was already opening the car door and said with relief, "I was wondering where they were. It's not like them to let a car arrive unannounced."

The two golden retrievers were still barking when they burst into the clearing and spotted their mistress. The barks and whines became apologetic, then welcoming. Neither paid any attention to Matt, who also slowly climbed out of the car.

Elena had crouched and was caressing the squirming dogs. "Dahlia, Daffy, did you miss me? I'll bet you're hungry dogs! Did you have a nice walk?" She dodged the wet tongues.

A sardonic voice made her look up. "Daffy?"

"It's Daffodil," she defended her choice. "Why not? They're gold, just like Daffy here, and it matches Dahlia, who I had first."

"Is 'why not' your answer to everything?" he inquired.

"Not everything," she said with a faint smile, "but it serves its purpose."

"Which is to avoid answering questions?"

"Sometimes," she agreed, studying him.

Matt's hair looked silver in the harsh white light, which drained the scene of color. With his gray suit and immobile expression, he could have been carved from stone, but for the glitter of his eyes. Even they for an instant made her think of mirrors, merely reflecting the artificial light, but the thought vanished as quickly as it had come. Matt was too positive a personality to be merely a reflector.

She shrugged off her fantasy and said, "How do you like my house?"

For several minutes he said nothing, merely studying the place, while Elena saw it through his eyes. It suddenly looked very small. The logs, which interlocked on each corner, had been stripped of bark, and the protective coats she had put on had maintained their pale color. Small paned windows were inset in the thick walls, as was the heavy front door, but this side of the cabin was shadowed by the overhang of the front porch. The sharply pitched roof, however, could be seen clearly, as could the large window that barely fit between the rafters and made her second floor so airy.

Matt finally shook his head, bemused. The lady was full of surprises, he thought. He found himself more intrigued by the moment. "How did you find this place?"

"I built it."

He shot her a look of incredulity. "All by yourself? Raised the rafters with one hand while you were whipping the logs up with the other?"

Her chin lifted slightly. "I had help. I do have friends, you know."

"I don't doubt that," he said quietly. "I'm just having difficulty picturing a modern-day house-raising."

"It hasn't changed much," she said with a glint of amusement. "Especially since I didn't have my electricity in at the time, so we couldn't use power tools. But I shouldn't run on about it. If you live in a condominium finished to the last detail, I don't imagine you can understand how satisfying it can be to work on your own place."

Matt raised one brow at the sudden display of prickliness, but he contented himself with a brief, "Don't underestimate me."

At that moment Dahlia decided to make friends with the stranger. She advanced on him, her entire body wriggling from her chest back to the tip of her plumed tail. Unfortunately, Elena had discovered while petting the dogs that they had found a mud hold in the woods, and their silky chests and feathered legs were filthy. She made a grab for Dahlia, but it was too late. The dog bumped against his legs, then pushed between them in her friendliest gesture. Elena cringed.

Unperturbed, however, Matt reached down and stroked the soft head, then leaned over so he could scratch Dahlia's throat and chest. He pulled back his hand, looked at it, then, with a shrug, resumed petting the dog. "This suit needed cleaning anyway."

Elena gazed at the top of his blond head, which looked as though it would be as silky to the touch as the golden retrievers' elegant fur. "I'm sorry." She was tired and felt curiously nervous. She didn't think she was up to having him in her house, appraising her meager possessions, but he had done her an enormous favor by bringing her home, so she owed him the courtesy of inviting him in. "Would you like to come in and have a cup of coffee?"

He looked up and flicked a glance first at the cabin, then at her. She knew her present appearance must seem incongruous in these surroundings. It must have been something of a shock for him to discover that the woman he had asked out was not what she seemed, that her expensive clothes were only a front for the T-shirt and jeans lurking beneath.

Elena wished she hadn't bowed to the undeniable physical attraction she felt for Matt and agreed to have dinner with him. That magnetism was still present, making her long for her customary composure. But now that they were totally alone, surrounded only by dark woods, she was more conscious than ever of his strong hands stroking the dog, of the easy way his muscles moved under his very civilized garments, of his mouth softening as his eyes met hers.

"Thank you," he finally replied, "but I think I'll pass on coffee. It's getting late, and I'm sure you don't need company." He hoped his regret didn't show. He'd pushed their acquaintance as far as he dared on this first date, given the circumstances. With a final pat on Dahlia's head, he straightened.

Elena hadn't realized how close she had come to him in her rush to stop Dahlia's friendly overtures. She had to restrain herself from taking a step back. Instead she managed to smile up at him, at the same time wishing he weren't so much taller than she, and held out her hand. "Thank you for dinner," she said. "And for the ride. You've been very kind. And I *am* sorry Dahlia got mud all over you. If you'd send me the—"

"Don't be ridiculous," he interrupted brusquely, dismayed by the finality in her tone. "I enjoyed your company, and the drive was no problem."

He took her hand and held it in a tight grip as he looked down at her face. He'd been wanting to kiss her all evening. Several times he had been so distracted by the soft curve of her lips that he'd lost the train of what she was saying. Now those lips were gently parted, and her eyes were wide and dark staring up at him. *Perhaps he could push just a little harder*, he thought, then quickly bent his head and pressed his lips against hers. His fingers were still closed on her hand, but he didn't force her in any way. He left his other hand at his side, and with an effort kept the touch of his mouth gentle and inquiring, not demanding.

At first Elena didn't respond, but then the excitement she had been keeping dammed up flooded through her body. Lips parted, she leaned toward him as though pulled by a magnetic force. Her free hand groped for him and closed on the smooth fabric of his jacket. She clung to both his hand and his jacket, needing the support to hold up her absurdly weak body.

For just an instant she felt his mouth pressing harder against hers, and his hand slid around to the small of her back, as if he meant to pull her against his muscular length. Then abruptly he released her, leaving her swaying, feeling chilled and dazed.

He stared down at her upturned face for a moment, his chest rising and falling at a rapid pace. In an odd tone he said, "Good night, Elena." With his fingertips he softly traced the line of her cheekbone. Then he turned away.

She stood, flanked by the dogs, as he climbed into the car, started it up and drove away. The sound of the engine faded quickly, muffled by the thick growth of trees.

The clearing was silent when Elena finally said aloud, explosively, "Damn!" and turned toward the protective shelter of her house.

3

"OH, FOR HEAVEN'S SAKE!" Elena muttered as the thin-walled bowl forming between her hands collapsed. In disgust she wadded the clay and threw it on her worktable with the remnants of her previous two projects. Her entire output from the morning's work consisted of one small, perfectly shaped bowl. Her satisfaction when she looked at its graceful lines was qualified by the fact that, although the bowl was beautiful, it wasn't at all what she'd had in mind for the upcoming Viking Art Show in the nearby town of Stanwood. But then, nothing she had accomplished in the past four days had come out as she'd intended. That, she told herself grimly, would teach her to let her thoughts dwell on a man whom she would most likely never see again!

Outwardly the week had been perfectly normal. Friends had visited. She had spent hours hoeing and weeding in her sprouting garden and had cleaned her house from top to bottom, including the windows. She'd told herself that this effort was simply the result of her normal spring cleaning instinct; it had nothing to do with her not wanting Matt to see her place in its usual comfortably messy state. She had glazed an accumulation of pots, loading and unloading her small kiln several times. And yet, the entire week she'd felt as though she were only going through the motions; her usual contentment had been inexplicably absent.

Now she took herself firmly in hand. One more try, she decided, separating a lump of clay from the mass she'd laboriously prepared first thing this morning. She plopped it on the plaster bat in the center of her wheel, then flicked the switch to set the wheel spinning. Concentrating, she worked with her hands to center the clay.

The wheel spun faster, and the squishy clay began to take shape. She drew it up into a cylinder, then began to force the center down with her thumbs to begin the hollowing-out process.

Slowly she pressed out and down with her thumbs. The sides began to thin and she widened the lip. This would be a small casserole. Elena envisioned it, complete with lid and handles, glazed with the new translucent blue she'd liked so well the first time she'd tried it. This would be a piece worthy of any art show.

A sound distracted her, and she lifted her head. Her hand jerked, causing a ripple to appear in the bowl's side, then the thin clay slumped inward. Completely frustrated, Elena switched off the wheel, shut her eyes and brushed a wisp of hair off her face with the back of her hand. What on earth was the matter with her? Normally she could shut out any extraneous thoughts when she was concentrating on her work. Today, though, she was as jumpy as a sparrow.

She listened. Someone had just come through her gate. The sound of the car motor was quite clear, until the dogs' barking drowned it. She walked out through the open door of her sun porch, speculating on who had decided to stop by her outpost.

A charcoal-gray Mercedes stood in the small clearing in front of her house. Matt's car. As she watched, frozen, the door opened. He climbed leisurely out and began rubbing the dogs' heads. They apparently remembered him and quieted immediately.

"Is your mistress home?" he asked the dogs, and then his gaze rose and he saw her. He nodded with a faint smile. "Hello, Elena. Are you busy?"

Her feet felt unconnected to her brain, and it took Elena a moment to reestablish command so that she could walk forward with an uncertain smile and say, "Hello, Matt." She didn't voice any of the astonished questions that filled her mind, but the air fairly quivered with them.

He looked quite different casually dressed. He still had that indefinable air of authority, though, as if he was incapable of relaxing completely. Elena would have expected Matt's notion of casual dress to be designer jeans and perhaps a simple yet expensive polo shirt. Instead he wore faded Levi's that clung to his muscular thighs and a plaid sport shirt. His sleeves were rolled up to expose brown forearms gilded with a wash of pale gold hair.

"Busy?" he repeated, his gaze inquiring.

Her hands were covered with wet clay, and she had been holding them out before her, palms forward, like a criminal surrendering. The clay was drying in the sun, and she could feel it tightening her skin. "I was potting. Well, actually, I was failing to pot. So it's nothing that can't wait."

He grinned. "You mean you occasionally fail?"

His teasing tone helped put her at her ease, and she wriggled her tense shoulders. "Even I, occasionally, fail," she admitted solemnly. "Come on in."

"You can go ahead with your work," he said as he followed her around the corner of the cabin. "I'll watch."

"No, that's fine. I'll just put the wet clay in a plastic bag and save it for another day. It wasn't going well today, anyway. I wasn't kidding." She sneaked a peek at his face from the corner of her eye. What on earth was he doing here? If he'd come about her loan he wouldn't have appeared on Saturday in old jeans and battered canvas tennis shoes. Besides, bankers didn't make house calls on clients who wanted a puny twenty-five-hundred-dollar loan.

She led him through the propped-open screen door and into what she called her sun porch; it was actually her workroom. He paused in the doorway and looked around with obvious curiosity.

"There's my wheel." She gestured toward the potter's wheel that stood at one end of the narrow room. As she had been interrupted in the middle of work, it was still covered with runny slips of the fine-textured red clay she had been using. At the other end of the room was a long, heavy table, where she kneaded her clay and glazed finished work.

"I can see why your mother likes your casseroles," Matt commented thoughtfully. He had moved over to the shelves that ran the length of the room and was studying a large piece with ornamental handles that she had glazed but not yet refired.

"Thank you," she said, but found herself wondering if he meant the compliment. After all, he'd surely felt obligated to say something nice.

At that thought she pulled herself up with a jerk. She was being absurd! She *was* a talented potter, so why doubt that Matt meant what he'd said?

Still chiding herself, she laid plastic over the one finished bowl, then put the wet ball of red clay into a bag and sealed the opening. Matt had propped one shoulder comfortably against the door frame and watched with unnerving intensity as she sat down at the wheel and picked up her sponge.

"I need to clean the wheel," she explained. "If I don't, the clay dries and it's harder to get up. If you don't keep your wheel really clean, you get little bits of dried clay in with the wet and it ruins what you're working on." She was sponging up the slop that was dripping off the wheel and lay in globs and pools in the metal tray underneath.

When she had wrung out the sponge for the last time, she sat back and looked at Matt, who was still lounging in the doorway. The sun streamed in around him, turning his light hair into a glistening halo. She settled on the direct approach and began, "Is this visit business or . . ."

When she hesitated Matt saw that a blush tinged her cheekbones. "Pleasure" was what she'd been going to say, and he couldn't help being pleased at her self-consciousness about using the word in a context that included him. He wasn't surprised when she immediately collected herself. Elena Simpson wasn't the woman to let herself be deflected so easily from her purpose.

"I don't want to be rude," she said in the forthright fashion that he associated with her, "but I'm wondering why you're here. I enjoyed myself the other night, but I got the definite impression that you didn't completely approve of me."

"Did you?" he remarked thoughtfully. "And all the time I had the impression that it was you who didn't approve of me."

He was interested to see that she responded not with embarrassment, but with a challenge. Her gray eyes didn't waver from his as she asked, "Did that bother you?"

"No," Matt said, although that wasn't strictly the truth. More honestly, he added, "I'm very attracted to you. And I like you." He offered his most persuasive smile. "I brought a picnic lunch with me. I thought we could eat out in the sun." When she didn't immediately answer, he coaxed, "The food's getting warm."

Elena shook her head and laughed, unable to deny the flutter of excitement that had leaped insistently to life the minute she saw his car. "A picnic sounds like fun," she said. "But I've absolutely got to shower and change clothes first. Look at me."

She always wore a pair of men's overalls when she worked and, as usual, they were caked with clay of several different consistencies. Even her old blue tennis shoes were covered with hardening clay. Her hands were stained rust-red and felt gritty when she wiped them on a rag. Elena was seldom self-conscious and as a rule regarded clothes as unimportant, mere trappings that either hid, or revealed, a person's true nature. For once, however, she wished she didn't work in such an incredibly ugly garment. She was surprised, looking as she did, that Matt had been able to stare her in the eye and say that he found her attractive.

"I've been looking," he returned with amusement. "This image does make quite a change from the other night. Why don't I put the wine in the refrigerator while you shower? You *do* have a refrigerator?"

She had been on her way into the main house, but at his words she abruptly stopped and swung around to face him. "Hey," she said, "I know this place looks primitive to you, but believe it or not the twentieth century *has* touched me."

Matt held her eyes steadily. "I'm sorry, Elena." He wasn't sure from her tone whether she was annoyed, but he wouldn't blame her if she was. Although his remark had been made in a teasing way, it *was* a jab—one that had sprung out of his subconscious. It made him wonder if she hadn't been right about his air of disapproval. Still thoughtful, he headed out the side door to his car.

After watching him go, Elena went on toward the bathroom, a tiny frown creasing her brow. She couldn't help but think it would be a mistake to let Matt into her life. It wouldn't be even remotely possible for them to develop an undemanding friendship, what with their different life-styles. No, never undemanding, she decided. There were too many sparks between them for so tepid a relationship to work. But why not friends? Or even, she thought with a quiver in her stomach, lovers.

She had laid out clean clothes in the bathroom as she always did before beginning work. She didn't like to paw through her closet or drawers with clay-covered hands or track any more of the stuff around than was unavoidable, especially when she had just cleaned the house.

She stripped quickly, dumping her overalls and shirt in the hamper. She didn't bother to wash them very often, but that earlier twinge of self-consciousness made her decide to try to keep them cleaner. One of these days, if she weren't careful, the clay would dry so hard she wouldn't be able to get out of them. Maybe she could sell herself as a sculpture.

She tilted her face up to the stream of hot water, letting it run over her body, then turned her back to the shower head so the water beat against her neck and between her shoulder blades. As she ran the bar of soap over her slippery skin, she found herself smiling, enjoying the sensations conjured up by the hot water streaming between her breasts, down over her belly and thighs, by her awareness of Matt Terrell's presence in the same house. The knowledge that she stood here naked and he was just beyond that closed door gave her a pleasurable consciousness of her body.

Suddenly Elena was anxious to be out of the shower. She wanted to be certain that he was indeed still around and hadn't decided after their last exchange to forget the whole thing and go home.

She quickly shampooed her hair, rinsed it, shut off the water and stepped out into the steamy, silent bathroom. She toweled dry her mass of honey-brown hair and hurriedly dressed in the waiting jeans and crisp red-

and-blue striped Oxford-cloth shirt, which she left unbuttoned far enough to hint at the first curves of her breasts. She was still combing out her hair when she padded barefoot into the kitchen.

A wicker basket sat in the middle of the wood table, and Matt lounged in one of her pressed-back kitchen chairs. He looked completely relaxed and at home. She smiled her relief and dragged a chair over to the window, where the sunlight would warm her still-damp hair.

He returned her smile, saying, "You look like a little girl. Sort of."

Elena noticed then that Pansy, one of her cats, had comfortably ensconced herself on Matt's lap. She lay draped across his thighs, with her head twisted to better expose the sensitive chin and throat that she loved to have scratched. He was obliging her obvious demand, and she was repaying him with her loud, strong purr.

"What's this one's name?" he asked.

Elena answered with a straight face. "Pansy."

"I should have known," he said with resignation.

"Well, you should have," she said laughingly. "See, look at where the sun's hitting her fur. Doesn't the color look like one of those dark pansies?" The cat's plush black fur did have a purplish cast in the sunlight, which had given Elena the inspiration for her name.

"Don't tell me," he said. "Do you have a Petunia, too?"

"Now you're getting the idea," she approved. "But actually I don't. I do have a Marigold, who is an orange kitty, and then there's Jamaal."

"Does that mean you're a Lakers fan?"

"Um-hm," she confirmed, shaking back her hair. For a moment she watched the practiced way his fingers moved in Pansy's fur. "Do you have any pets?"

"Actually I do." Matt looked out the window at the long, tangled grass, the apple trees and the weathered gray side of the shed. "I have a cat called Leander. I was just thinking how much he'd love it here. I don't, contrary to your delightful opinion of me, live in a condominium, but my yard's not very big. Leander, intelligently, is so scared of cars he doesn't venture far from home. He'd go crazy here."

"Bring him for a visit," Elena offered impulsively. "Jamaal's my only male, and he's not very aggressive. He's only a year old, anyway. I think he'd be friendly."

"Maybe I will." His smile caressed her. "Probably neither of us would want to go home."

She curled her toes against the rough wood of the kitchen floor and looked away from his seductive smile. "I'm ready for that picnic," she said brightly, getting to her feet. "Can I provide anything?"

"Just your beautiful self." He gently deposited Pansy on the floor and rose, too. "Why don't you put some shoes on, and we'll get this show on the road?"

Elena followed his advice and on an impulse left her long hair loose. It fell nearly to her waist and to keep it out of her way she usually wore it braided or in a coil at her nape. Having it swing about her shoulders at her every movement made her feel free, even a little provocative.

They laid out the blanket he had brought in the shade of a big apple tree that stood beside the creek. The shallow, running water made sparkling patterns that shifted and danced before their eyes, and it was deep enough to dangle feet in. With the air of a conjuror, Matt produced from his basket the cooled bottle of white Moselle wine, two wineglasses, baked chicken breasts, several varieties of cheese, French bread, crisp red Delicious apples and two slices of apple strudel, which he said was from his local bakery.

"You mean you put this together?" she asked incredulously, peering into the basket, where she discovered a plastic bag filled with lengths of carrot, celery and cucumber. "It's enough for six people!"

He grinned. "I thought you might have a big appetite."

She brandished a stick of celery at him. "Are you implying that I look like I eat a lot?"

He eyed her slender figure thoughtfully. "You know better than that. But maybe I should see a little more before I reach a final judgment."

She made an offhand rejoinder, hoping he couldn't see how powerfully his teasing affected her and how her body was reacting to those sensuous looks. She had a feeling of unreality when she looked at him and recalled her first impression. He was stretched out on his side, head propped on one hand. His eyes were half-closed; he gazed reflectively at the creek. He seemed comfortable with the long silence between them. She sensed none of the wariness and tension that had seemed so strong in him at their first meeting; rather, he looked totally relaxed and contented.

Elena was sitting cross-legged on the blanket, sipping her wine and nibbling at the corner of the strudel. Suddenly she said, "Uh-oh."

Matt looked at her with raised brows.

"Here come the scavengers." She nodded toward the house.

Pansy, who had initially scorned their company, probably because she was offended at being displaced from that wonderful lap, was making a casual approach, trailed by Jamaal. Their sights were clearly set on the chicken.

"Gluttons," Matt grumbled as he shredded scraps of chicken for the cats.

Elena just laughed. "They may be gluttons," she said, "but you're a sucker."

Now the dogs, who had been lying in the shade and confining themselves to wistful glances, rose to their feet and edged closer to the blanket. Elena had trained them not to beg, but seeing the cats making off with the goodies was more than they could stand. In the end, most of the chicken went to the animals.

The afternoon passed faster than Elena would have believed possible. The shade crept back, leaving their blanket in the sun. The warmth made them both feel languorous; their conversation was desultory, with long, sleepy pauses.

Finally Matt groaned and sat up. "I should be going," he said. "Unfortunately, I have some plans I can't change."

Elena let pass his easy assumption that she would have spent the evening with him if he had been free, because it was true. She wondered what his unbreakable plans involved. Perhaps he had a date with some sophisticated woman, who fit with ease into his world. And what of it? She scolded herself for having forgotten over the course of the afternoon how different their lives were. The picture that had formed in her mind of him in that expensive gray suit with a lovely, elegant woman at his side reminded her again how little they had in common.

She realized that he was looking expectantly at her, as though waiting for her to speak. Unable to prevent the blush that crept into her cheeks, she attempted to collect herself. "I'm sorry," she murmured. "Did you say something?"

Matt looked at her quizzically. "You were staring straight at me," he said. "I asked you to a cocktail party next Friday. We'll have dinner afterward, of course, but this is one of those affairs I can't afford to miss. It's at the bank president's home."

She blinked. "A cocktail party? That's not exactly my style, Matt. Can you picture me?"

She sat on the edge of the creek, shoes beside her and jeans rolled up almost to her knees, her feet in the water. Her shirttail hung loose, and there were grass stains on elbows, a smudge of dirt on her cheek.

Matt laughed. "Not at the moment. But I saw you the other day. You can look different if you choose."

Elena rolled her eyes. "I'm afraid you mean 'better.'"

There was a little smile on his face as Matt lowered his eyes to the open neckline of Elena's blouse. "I wouldn't say that," he said gently. "You look sexy as hell like that."

Pink again touched Elena's cheeks. Her eyes edged away from his and she said uncertainly, "I don't know, Matt. I enjoyed this afternoon, but . . ."

Perplexed by her response, Matt waited for an explanation that didn't come. Perhaps it was arrogant of him, but after such a pleasant afternoon he couldn't believe that she didn't want to see him again as much as he wanted to see her. After a moment he said quietly, "I have to go, and I'd enjoy your company."

Elena met his steady gaze and felt herself nodding. Just because similar parties she had attended during her own brief business career had been offensive didn't mean this one would be equally objectionable. Maybe she would find she liked the people Matt worked with, and the conversation might be stimulating. And getting dressed up certainly wouldn't hurt her!

"I'm sorry," she said with a little shake of the head. "I don't know what's gotten into me! Of course I'd like to go, Matt! I'll look forward to it."

Matt reached out and tilted her chin up. "Good. Now, if you'll just leap at my invitation next time . . ."

Elena's pulse fluttered at the sensuous light in his eyes, but she crinkled her nose and managed to tease, "One step at a time, buddy. Don't push me."

Matt released her chin to tap her nose with one finger. "Better watch your words! I might take that as a challenge."

Deciding that discretion was the better part of valor, Elena didn't respond. Matt just laughed. In companionable silence, they repacked his wicker basket and folded the blanket. He waited while she put on her tennis shoes, and then they walked slowly back to the car.

Matt opened the door, then turned to her. "I enjoyed myself today."

She smiled. "I'm glad you came, Matt. I didn't expect to see you again, and . . . It was nice."

He stepped closer to her and began to trace the line of her jaw with one gentle finger. "Could we get together during the week, Elena?" he asked softly. "Would you have lunch with me when you pick up your car?"

She nodded. Her body had begun to tremble with anticipation and from the impact of his feather-light touch. She felt like a rabbit mesmerized by oncoming headlights, unable to walk away or turn her back on her reaction to Matt.

When his hands closed on her shoulders and he pulled her toward him, she tilted back her head, lips parted to meet his hungry kiss. The kiss quickly deepened, their embrace became urgent. His arms encircled her and pressed her against his hard body, while his mouth moved with increasing insistence against hers. But as demanding as his touch was, Elena felt the underlying tenderness, and it was this that heated her blood and made her response so unrestrained.

Groaning, he lifted his head and looked down at her with glittering eyes. "Damn," he finally muttered. "I wish I didn't have to go."

Her breath was coming fast and she could hear her own pulse hammering in her ears, but Elena managed to summon enough possession to step back, away from him. "Maybe it's just as well." She strove for a tranquil smile and added, "I'll see you later this week. Friday for sure."

He regarded her for a moment, then apparently accepted her decision. "Sure. I'll call you, Elena." A quick smile flitted across his face. "Say goodbye to Pansy. I made a real hit there."

She chuckled. "Don't get smug. Maybe she'll scratch you the next time you come."

When he had gone and she could no longer hear the sound of his car's engine, Elena found it hard to believe he had really been there. If she had been at loose ends before—unable to concentrate—well, how much worse it would be now! She was glad she had agreed to go to the cocktail party despite her doubts. At least she could be certain that she would see him again.

OVER THE NEXT several days, Elena tried to put thoughts of Matt out of her mind, having discovered that she would otherwise get little done. Unfortunately, determinedly *not* thinking about him was as bad as doing so. And there were far too many unwary moments when she would find herself picturing him. With photographic clarity, she recalled the sight of him on her doorstep: faded jeans molded to the long muscles of his legs, shirt-sleeves rolled up to expose strong brown forearms, gray eyes narrowed with a mixture of amusement and sensual awareness.

So when he called on Wednesday morning to let her know her bank loan had been approved and to ask her out to lunch, she agreed without a moment's hesitation. That left her with the necessity of begging a ride, but luckily her friend Sallie was going into town to restock some supplies. Elena barely had time to put plastic over the pot she'd been working on and to change clothes before the arrival of her friend's pickup was announced by the dogs.

When Sallie dropped her at the bank, Elena walked briskly to the door. Once inside, she went directly over to the secretary who sat in front of Matt's office. She could see him beyond, through the glass, his blond head bent over some papers and a frown of concentration on his face.

The dark-haired woman who sat behind the desk looked up from her calculator. "Can I help you?"

She smiled. "I'm Elena Simpson. I believe Mr. Terrell is expecting me."

"Oh, yes." The older woman returned her smile with more cordiality than she might have if Elena hadn't changed from her normal jeans and clay-daubed tennis shoes to blue poplin slacks, a summery, short-sleeved turquoise print blouse and low-heeled Swedish clogs. "I have your check right here." She handed over a long envelope, which Elena slipped into the pocket of her purse. "And I'm sure Mr. Terrell won't mind being interrupted. Go right in."

"Thank you." Elena stepped past the woman's desk. With her hand on the doorknob, however, she paused, looking past the gilt letters that announced Matt's name. The total attention he was giving to his work allowed her to study him unnoticed through the glass.

She realized uncomfortably that today he was the complete banker—the epitome of restraint, from his well-cut, dark-gray suit and discreet tie to the taut planes of his face. With the glint in his light gray eyes shielded by lowered lids and his mobile mouth compressed in a straight line, one would never have guessed at any other facets of his nature. Elena could scarcely connect him to the man who had lounged so contentedly in her kitchen chair, stroking her cat while he bandied light words with her.

She opened the door. At the click of the latch he looked up. Something quickened behind his eyes and he stood abruptly but with the easy grace that hinted at the strength disguised by his tailored suit. Elena's uneasiness subsided, replaced by that quiver of awareness he'd evoked in her from their first meeting.

Sensing Elena's instant of wariness, Matt smiled with deliberate charm as he circled the desk. "I'm glad you could make it, Elena," he said warmly. The conventional words sounded merely polite, but were truer than she could know. He'd thought she might change her mind and decide not to come after all. The fact that she had misgivings where he was concerned was all too obvious.

"One of my neighbors gave me a ride," she said, taking his comment at face value. "Sallie's a good friend of mine. She's a potter, too."

He lifted his brows. "You fraternize with the competition?"

Elena laughed. "Don't you?"

Matt's tone was sardonic. "Very carefully, I assure you." He gestured toward the door. "Shall we go?"

After exchanging a few words with his secretary, Matt ushered her out of the bank. After starting the Mercedes, he glanced at Elena. "I thought we might go to the Cabbage Patch. Unless you have another suggestion?"

"No, that's fine," she assured him, although he saw the surprise on her face. It amused him to speculate on what restaurant she'd expected him to choose. Presumably the Cabbage Patch didn't jibe with her image of him.

Actually, it was one of his favorite places to eat—friendly and unpretentious. Established before the dolls had made the name a household word, the restaurant was situated in an old, red-painted two-story house. Diners were seated in any of several small rooms or odd cubbyholes including, in warm weather, a glassed-in back porch. The unpolished wood floors were bare, and the furniture was a hodgepodge of old carved oak pieces. Much of the Cabbage Patch's special atmosphere came from the collection of antiques and curios displayed in every room: an old-fashioned scale, advertisements from early in the century, fringed lamps and stained glass that hung in the windows.

Elena and Matt were seated in a back room, which they had to themselves. After studying the newsprint menu for only a moment, Matt decided on a potato stuffed with crab, while Elena chose a half sandwich and the spicy minestrone soup that carried the restaurant's name.

As the waitress walked away with the menus, Matt remarked, "At least after eating here, I can usually skip dinner. And considering my lack of enthusiasm for cooking, that's a good thing."

Somehow his comment didn't surprise Elena. It was difficult to picture the man who sat across from her in a domestic guise, complete with apron and spatula. On the other hand, she'd misjudged him before. Her guess that he had never dipped hands in dishwater and wouldn't know what to do with a vacuum cleaner might well be wrong.

"I know what you mean," she agreed. Although she did love cooking on occasion, producing daily meals became tiresome. "It's not much fun for one person."

A broad smile lit his face. "We'll just have to fill up, then," he said. "If I'm not mistaken, I saw some home-made peach cobbler in that glass case on the way in."

"I had my eye on the blueberry pie," she admitted.

He gave a mock bow. "Your wish is my command."

They grinned at each other and warmth filtered through Elena. Each time she saw Matt smile, she was startled afresh by the change in his face, which otherwise held a look of such cool reserve. She wondered, not for the first time, which expression most closely represented the real Matt.

She propped her elbows on the table and said seriously, "Tell me something about yourself, Matt. You know way more about me than I do about you."

Amusement showed in his eyes. "I thought you had me pegged right down to the architecture of my condominium."

Elena made a rueful face. "Your nonexistent condominium. But, hey, anybody can get a few details wrong."

The laugh lines around Matt's gray eyes became even more pronounced. "Ah-ha! The lady gives herself away! So you do think you have me pegged."

She hesitated before carefully choosing her words. "I wouldn't put it that strongly, but I imagine I could make some pretty good guesses about your background."

Still smiling, his eyes not leaving her face, Matt leaned back in his chair and with one hand worked his tie loose, drawing her gaze to the strong column of his throat. At last he said, "Guess away, then. I'll correct you. We'll make it a true or false quiz."

Elena looked at him uncertainly. "Are you sure?"

"I'm sure." His tone was positive, reflecting his satisfaction with the turn the conversation had taken. Not that he was his own favorite subject, but something told him Elena would reveal more of herself in speculating about his life than she would in offering a carefully edited version of her own. He might find out at last what it was about him that made her so nervous.

After the barest of pauses, she gave him a crooked smile. "I think you just want to embarrass me. But I guess I was asking for it, wasn't I? So, okay, here goes. I picture you as growing up in the all-American family, father a professional, mother a housewife, two-point-two kids, or whatever the average is supposed to be."

"Not bad so far," he conceded. "Except for the point two, which would be tough to achieve. I have a sister, my father's an architect, Mom went to college but never worked."

Just then the waitress set their soup bowls in front of them, but Matt wasn't about to let her off the hook. He picked up his spoon and nodded at her. "Go on. This is just getting interesting."

Elena saw the challenge in his eyes and her chin lifted a little in response. She took a deliberately long moment to savor the spicy soup before she continued confidently, "You went to some terrific private college, where you majored in . . . oh, maybe economics. Then you got an MBA."

"Actually," he corrected, "I went to the University of Washington and majored in history. I also played basketball. I'll bet you never saw me as the athletic type."

Her gaze fleetingly took in the breadth of his shoulders before she looked back to her soup. "You *are* well-built," she stated, hoping she sounded more matter-of-fact than she felt.

"Thank you," he returned gravely. "You have a very nice build yourself."

Elena's cheeks suddenly felt warm, not because of the gentle mockery in his tone, but because of the way he was regarding her. She made herself sit completely still, as though unaware of his appraisal. With false nonchalance, she returned, "Thank *you*. Tell me, was I right about the MBA?"

There was a knowing spark of humor in his eyes, but he answered obligingly, "Yes, from Stanford."

"Hah!" she crowed. "I knew there was a private school in there somewhere."

He paused with the spoon halfway to his mouth. "What made you so sure?"

"Oh, the clothes," she explained airily. She waved her hand to take in the white shirt, which had a sheen that told her it wasn't from J.C. Penney's, the conservative dark-green silk tie and the gray suit jacket that fit his wide shoulders with no trace of a sag or wrinkle. "The look is so smooth. You didn't learn to dress like that at a state school."

"Did it ever occur to you," he mocked, amusement softening his features, "that my handsome suit has more to do with my income than my background? After all, you know how much money we bankers leech out of the community. Nothing but the best for us."

The conflicting emotions on her face told him his arrow had found its mark. Whatever the roots of her prejudice, bankers obviously didn't rate high in her estimation. He found himself oddly gratified, however, at the restraint she showed in not rising to his bait. All she said was a light, "That could be it," plainly leaving it to him to guess whether she was serious.

He grinned to let her know he'd read her mind, but their conversation was interrupted by the waitress bringing the rest of their lunch.

Elena pulled the toothpick from her sandwich and gave an unnecessary degree of attention to peeling a slice of orange. It was disconcerting to find herself so flustered every time Matt directed that warm, knowing smile her way. In one way it was exhilarating, of course, but it was also decidedly alarming. However much she enjoyed his company, she still knew little about Matt Terrell, and much of what she did know placed him at odds with her.

She had finished her orange when he suggested, "If we can leave the subject of my wardrobe behind, you're welcome to take on the rest of my life. And then next time," he added casually, "we'll turn the tables."

Elena stiffened. "But I've already told you about my background," she protested. "In fact, too much! I don't make a habit of baring my soul that way."

"I guessed that," he said quietly. "But you did leave out a few basics. At which—" his sudden grin was the tiniest bit malicious "—I think I can take an educated guess. After all—"

She groaned. "Don't even say it. Well, I guess I'd better enjoy myself while I can. So, let's see." She thought for a moment. "You must be in your thirties,

so I'll bet you're married and divorced. That is," she
added with a twinge of alarm, "I hope divorced."

Matt's brows rose. "Did you think I'd ask you out if
I was married?"

Elena gave a shrug. "You wouldn't be the first man
to have ideas like that," she said cheerfully. "But since
you ask, no, I didn't think you were married. I figured
you wouldn't have invited me to your boss's reception
if you were."

She held his narrowed gaze with an amused one of
her own, and at length his mouth tilted into a reluctant
smile and wry humor showed in his eyes.

"That's not what I was hoping to hear," he said dryly.
"I thought my sterling character was so obvious that
you'd have noticed it by now."

Elena dropped her sandwich on her plate. "Matt," she
said frankly, "I like you. I wouldn't be sitting here if I
didn't. But I hardly know you. I don't think you can be
sure what I'd do or not do any more than I know the
same about you. Besides," she added on a lighter note,
"you haven't answered my question."

Throughout her little speech he'd watched her with
shuttered eyes, leaving her with no idea what he was
thinking. Now he picked up his fork. "If I remember
your statement correctly," he said, and there was a glint
in his eyes that told her he did, "the answer is no marriage, no divorce. And," he added as a seeming after-
thought, "I'm thirty-two."

"How come?" Elena asked on impulse.

His smile suddenly held genuine amusement again.
"Well, I'd have to say my parents had something to do
with that. They must have had a particularly intimate

evening around about...oh, April of..." He appeared to be giving the date serious thought.

Elena wrinkled her nose at him. "You know what I mean."

His shoulders moved in an easy shrug. "Would you believe I never met the right woman?"

"That depends on whether it's the truth."

Matt regarded her pensively over the rim of his glass as he took a sip of water. "I think it is," he said at last.

Elena knew disbelief must show on her face. It was in her voice, as well, when she said skeptically, "You've never even been close?"

"I didn't say that," he reminded her gently. He then proceeded to take a bite of his potato and began to chew with frustrating slowness.

He obviously had no intention of elaborating. But then, what business did she have grilling him, anyway? None, she told herself firmly, taking a bite of her own sandwich.

Only then did Matt put down his fork and continue matter-of-factly, "I did almost ask a woman to marry me once. It was a few years ago. Fortunately, I thought better of it in time. It wasn't really her I wanted, not for the rest of my life. I was just in a marrying mood."

Elena could understand that. Living by oneself was often lonely and the temptation could be great to settle for whomever was available. She'd had her moments, too. And in Matt's case, he likely viewed a wife as a desirable asset to his career, which would bring added pressure.

That thought produced another in its wake. At least she didn't need to worry that he was interested in her because he was again in a marrying mood; as wife material, she doubtlessly fell well on the debit side of his ledger! An undisciplined potter who lived in a log cabin with a bunch of animals and preferred never to change out of her blue jeans must be a far cry from the elegant woman he probably imagined gracing his life. In fact, Elena was certain the instant attraction that had flared between them had been as much of a shock to him as it had to her. Even now a special awareness seemed to shimmer in the air between them, a compelling force that neither could ignore.

She looked down at the remnant of her sandwich, avoiding his contemplative look. "So why are you in Snohomish, Washington," she asked, "and not on Wall Street? Couldn't you get a job?"

Matt gasped theatrically and pressed one hand to his chest. "A knife to the heart! You know how to wound a man, don't you?"

"Is your male ego so sensitive?" she inquired sweetly.

He laughed. "I had offers, but when it came right down to it I didn't want to live in New York or even stay in the San Francisco Bay area. I grew up here in Washington, and I like it. I'm not ruling out a move later on, if my ambitions get the best of me." He gave her a mocking grin. "For the moment I'm satisfied."

She was curious. "Aren't you young to be vice president of a bank?"

"I suppose." He shrugged. "I'm good at my job."

He sounded not so much arrogant as certain, and Elena had no trouble accepting that. She knew her own skill at the wheel, too, just as during her abortive career in business she'd known she lacked the necessary spark. And she had no difficulty believing that Matt was superb at his job; he wore so naturally an air of confidence, which was both tempered and accentuated by his inner control and his sense of humor.

At the same time, his very certainty disturbed Elena, because of the nature of his job. She wandered if he ever hesitated over a decision that would crush someone's hopes, if he saw things entirely in terms of profit and loss.

She couldn't help asking, "Aren't there things about your job you find repugnant?"

Matt looked at her sharply. Although her tone had been studiously neutral, the way she had phrased the question told him a great deal about her attitude. He wondered for an instant if there was any point in answering, if she would listen with an open mind. Well, if she didn't, there was nothing he could do about it. All he could do was try to tell her honestly how he felt.

"I take it you mean foreclosing and suchlike," he said. "Sure, there have been a few occasions when I've had to do something I felt badly about. For the most part, no. I was raised to believe people shouldn't borrow money unless they could pay it back, so I have very little sympathy for the kind of individual who doesn't think a thing about missing payments or overdrawing an account. And although I'm sometimes sorry to have to turn down a loan application, I don't believe it would be a kindness to give money to someone who in my judgment doesn't have the means to pay it back."

"How about someone who's been laid off from their job?" she challenged. "Does that constitute irresponsibility, too?"

"Not at all," he answered levelly. "We really aren't anxious to throw people out of their homes, you know. In fact, we go to extraordinary lengths not to if someone has a good credit record and the situation is out of their control. We have clients now who are six and eight months behind on their mortgage payments, but we think they're good risks and that someday we'll get our money back. With the lumber industry so low, there are hardworking people out of jobs, but we're doing our best not to make a bad situation worse."

Elena was studying him, her expression doubtful but also a little puzzled, as though he'd surprised her. Her look of enchanting earnestness made him want to laugh, and then kiss her. Either of which, he suspected, would be fatal at the moment.

At last she said, "You have an answer for everything, don't you?"

He spread his hands in a gesture of innocence. "Only the truth."

There was an almost infinitesimal pause before she conceded, saying, "Maybe."

Matt struggled with a smile. He was more amused than offended by Elena's grudging acceptance of his side of the story, mainly because he could see he'd gotten through to her. She might not want to believe in his good intentions, but his sincerity had plainly given her food for thought. And he was more than satisfied with that.

So he smiled and said in an altered tone, "Now, how about that blueberry pie?"

Elena found her own lips curving in response as she gladly acceded to Matt's effort to change the mood. "I think I could manage that," she admitted, so Matt signaled the waitress, who a moment later brought their desserts.

"Tell me more about yourself," Elena said. "So far, all you've given me are a few statistics. What's your family like?"

Matt looked surprised, as though he didn't realize how unrevealing he'd been, but obligingly began to reminisce about his childhood, which had obviously been a happy one. He told her that his sister had been a basketball player, as well.

"We're still close," he said, his fondness apparent. "I think you'd like Sheila. She's convinced being a banker has made me stuffy. She's an interior designer now, and I'll tell you, her interiors are the opposite of stuffy! She did my living room, by the way." He pretended to shudder. "I still haven't gotten used to it. I'm not sure it's me."

Elena chuckled. "Are you trying to tell me gray isn't the predominant color?"

Amusement sparked in his eyes. "Is that an insult?"

"Not at all," she said with mock dignity. "Just an observation. You wear gray clothes, your car's gray, even your eyes are gray." She paused, then asked suspiciously, "What about your cat?"

"Gray," he admitted ruefully. "But Leander was an accidental acquisition. And I couldn't help the eyes."

"I'll concede that," Elena agreed. "Nonetheless—"

He held up one hand. "Your point's made. Next time I see you, I'll wear red."

She suppressed a smile. "Great! That'll liven up your boss's cocktail party."

"Oh, Lord," Matt groaned. "I'd forgotten that. Would you settle for a nice red tie?"

She arched her brows. "Do you have one?"

"Well . . . maybe maroon."

"Yeah, that's what I figured," she teased. "Forget it. Gray suits you, anyway." To her discomfiture, her last words came out more sincerely than she'd intended, undoubtedly because they were true. The neutral colors he wore had the effect of highlighting his physical magnetism, rather like the white mat around a vibrant painting.

The corners of Matt's mouth twitched. "I'm not sure whether that's a compliment."

Elena's gaze met his. "It is," she said quietly.

They stared at each other across the small cluttered table, neither moving, until he murmured huskily, "Then, thank you."

She heard herself answer just as softly, "You're welcome," and still their gazes clung. His gray eyes glowed with an odd smoky light that made Elena's breath come faster. A tingling sensation spread through her body. Matt's stillness told her that he was as caught up in the moment as she, that the intensity of his look was not in her imagination.

Suddenly the white-aproned waitress was beside the table, and the spell was broken. The woman laid down the bill and began gathering dishes with a clatter while saying cheerfully, "How was everything? Oh, good. Well, I'll be your cashier when you're ready."

Their gazes clung for another instant, even as Matt assured the waitress the meal was fine and pulled his wallet from his pocket. Only at the necessity of count-

ing money onto the table did he look away, leaving
Elena to blink down at her empty dessert plate and
draw several slow, deep breaths. After a moment she
became aware again of the chatter and bustle around
them. Collecting her purse, she smiled with her usual
composure at the waitress.

On the way out to the car they didn't speak, although Matt took her arm in a firm grip as they made
their way up the cracked, uneven sidewalk. Once in the
car, he started the engine before glancing at her. "Can
I drop you at the car dealership?"

"Yes, thank you."

As he backed the Mercedes out of the slot, Matt
commented matter-of-factly, "I hope you don't have
any trouble driving that thing. A Volkswagen bus can
be a real bear."

"I did test-drive it," she reminded him. "Anyway, the
gearshift is pretty much the same as poor old Bessie's."

"Has she been gutted yet?" he asked.

Elena made a face. "I don't even want to think about
it. I always cry when I have to give up an old car."

He gave her a sidelong look. "Do you really?"

"I'm afraid so."

Matt laughed. "Well, here we are." He stopped the car
at the curb in front of Import Motors. "Would you like
me to wait, just in case there's a foul-up?"

"Heavens, no!" she exclaimed, opening the door.
"They're expecting me. In fact, there's my new bus,
right there." She pointed at the van, painted a sky blue.
"Thank you for lunch," she added sincerely.

"My pleasure." He was smiling, his eyes holding hers.
"I'll see you Friday? About five-thirty?"

"I'll be ready," she assured him as she climbed out. "Bye."

She waved as the Mercedes moved smoothly into traffic, then turned, smiling, to enter the grimy cement building. She'd enjoyed herself today, despite a moment or two of tension. It might even be, she thought, that those occasional disagreements added spice to her time with Matt. Well, if that was so, her date with him on Friday would definitely be interesting!

5

ELENA STOOD beside the sweep of floor-to-ceiling windows and watched as Matt effortlessly made his way through the crowd toward the bar. And *effortless* was definitely the operative word, she thought with a certain wry amusement. Others might have had to use their elbows or squirm through small openings, but for Matt the crowd parted like the Red Sea.

Even in this group of self-assured people Matt stood out. It was partly a result of his sheer physical magnetism. He was several inches taller than most of the other men present and the lithe grace of his movements, coupled with his broad shoulders and tautly muscled body, further separated him from them. But the potency of his presence was far from entirely physical. The force of his personality radiated from his silver-gray eyes and he had charisma that had turned heads when he'd walked into the room. Comparing him with the men he'd paused to talk with was like looking at some pretty travel posters next to an Ansel Adams black-and-white photograph. The posters would have nice colors, but you'd take in all there was to see in a glance. The photo, on the other hand, would have subtlety and infinite shades—depth and drama that drew the eye again and again.

Now she was getting fanciful, Elena chided herself, deliberately turning her back on the packed, noisy room that was enveloped in a haze of cigarette smoke. The view through the windows was such a contrast she longed to be outside, walking across the velvety lawn down to the lakeshore, perhaps taking off her sandals and sheer nylons so she could sit on the weathered wood dock and dip her bare feet in the chill water. She imagined Matt beside her and had to chuckle at the picture of him carelessly dropping those expensive Italian shoes on the grass and rolling up his finely tailored pants.

The president of Matt's bank lived on Lake Stevens, his enormous, ultramodern house sitting commandingly astride a point that thrust into the lake from the western shore. Through the glass Elena could see across the deep blue lake, now shrouded in early evening shadow. Beyond, the green-cloaked foothills and the jagged, snow-tipped Cascade Mountains were shining with unreal clarity in the last sunlight and seemed to hover just beyond the water.

Elena took a sip of the cool white wine she'd accepted from a waiter, her eyes still fixed on the mountains. She could easily imagine what it must have been like here when the woods were wild and only ducks cut a wake in the water. Now houses were packed like eggs in a carton along the shoreline and lawns as plush as the carpet of grass under her feet had replaced the tangle of natural vegetation.

"Enjoying our view?" a woman's voice inquired.

Elena turned to see her hostess, whom she'd met briefly at the front door when she and Matt had arrived. Frances Duncan was a tall woman, thin to the point of appearing brittle inside her red silk tunic and pants. Her short dark hair was touched with silver. She was smiling, but her eyes studied Elena with curiosity.

"It's lovely," Elena answered sincerely. "You're lucky to live here."

"It was always a dream of mine," Frances replied, though her attention seemed to be focused more on Elena than the beauty outside. "Do you live in the area, too?"

"I have a log house on some acreage beyond Snohomish," Elena replied. "Not as beautiful as this—" she waved toward the window "—but I enjoy my woods."

The older woman's dark brows rose in apparent surprise, and her voice warmed with interest. "A log house? Why, how interesting! It sounds charming."

Elena smiled. "I think it is. It's quite small, though, and lacking a few amenities. Some people might not agree with you."

Frances Duncan waved one hand dismissively. "Charm and practicality are two different things. Does your house suit you?"

Elena answered without hesitating. "Yes. Yes, it does. Does that tell you I'm not very practical?"

The other woman smiled. "Not necessarily. I don't believe Matt said what you do for a living."

"I'm a potter."

"That's fascinating." Frances was looking her over now, her frankly interested gaze taking in Elena's moss-green silk dress, which draped softly over the subtle curves of her slender figure. The silk was shot with silver threads, so that the fragile fabric shimmered as

Elena moved and the delicate folds reformed to her contours. Finally she remarked, somewhat baldly, "You don't look the part."

Elena wondered with amusement what the other woman thought she should be wearing. A gunnysack and work boots? Just because she seldom dressed up didn't mean she couldn't enjoy doing so occasionally. And any qualms she'd had about wearing this dress left from a past she'd put behind her had vanished the moment she'd opened her front door for Matt this evening.

His smile of greeting had died when he saw her, and his gaze had moved over her with an intensity that held her breathlessly still. When he'd looked at her face his eyes had darkened with a desire so unmistakable she'd suddenly felt her pulse racing. They had stared at each other for a frozen instant, Elena clutching the door for support and Matt a step below. And then at last he'd said in a husky voice, "You're beautiful." He hadn't kissed her or even touched her beyond holding her elbow lightly to help her over the rough ground to the car, but that look in his eyes was one Elena wanted never to forget. For an instant she had felt like a woman in the sweetest sense of the word, and for that it was worth wearing a dress in which she no longer felt altogether comfortable.

"I wonder if we aren't all more complex than we appear," she said thoughtfully.

To her surprise, the other woman agreed. "Oh, yes! You should see me in some of my other guises! But . . . well, never mind." She hesitated, then asked tentatively, "Tell me, how did you meet Matt? Or am I being too inquisitive?"

"Not at all," Elena returned politely. "Actually, it was in the bank. I applied for a loan and . . ." She shrugged and smiled.

Frances chuckled. "I should have known. I sometimes think the bank is the center of the universe! But maybe Sam has just infected me with his thinking! It happens when you've been married for a while, you know."

Elena did know and wasn't sure she liked the idea that a wife simply took on her husband's opinions. She was glad when Frances changed the subject. "My husband and I have known Matt for a long time. We consider him a dear friend."

Elena smiled. "I'm sure he feels the same. And speak of the devil . . ."

Matt arrived at her side just in time to overhear this last provocative remark. "Am I the devil?" he asked.

Elena gave him a flirtatious smile. "Isn't that a compliment?" she inquired with mock alarm. "I thought all men liked to be thought of that way."

Matt grinned. "Maybe . . . by the right woman." He imbued his tone with significance, eager to see how she'd respond. This Elena was new to him, a delicious counterpoint to her usual straightforward self.

He wasn't disappointed. She lowered her thick lashes demurely and murmured, "Oh, I'm so sorry. I didn't mean to intrude on sacred territory." Then her lashes swept back up to reveal laughter.

Their eyes held for just an instant, communicating amusement and a hint of deeper emotion that exhilarated Matt. Then he turned politely to Frances. "I hope you had a chance to get to know Elena."

"Yes, indeed." She gave Elena a friendly smile. "Elena was telling me about her log cabin, and being a potter. I hope I have a chance to see her work someday soon. Perhaps you could both come for dinner when Sam and I get back from vacation."

Both Elena and Matt accepted immediately, and she continued, "Please excuse me now. I'm afraid I've been enjoying myself so much I've neglected my other guests." She moved away, leaving Matt and Elena behind in a small eddy of silence.

After a moment Matt asked, "Did you like her?"

To his relief, Elena's response was a warm "very much." He'd been apprehensive about tonight, knowing he'd dragooned her into it. What he had feared, he wasn't sure, but nothing bad had yet to come to pass. Elena hadn't mixed much, but she seemed comfortable in the midst of these people. What's more, in that dress she reminded him of the delicate mosses that swayed from tree branches in the rain forest. She was breathtakingly lovely. And he wasn't the only man in the room fascinated by her every graceful move.

Her slender body wasn't all that fascinated him, though. Their conversation on the drive there had been as stimulating as any he could recall having had in a long while. He'd asked her casually if she liked to read, not letting on how important the answer was to him. He'd always found it a benchmark moment in the development of any friendship, perhaps because people whose minds were closed to the wealth of knowledge and adventure and sheer beauty in books seemed alien to him.

Elena had answered matter-of-factly, "That's like asking if I like to breathe! I'm one of those people who reads while I'm cooking, eating, brushing my teeth, waiting at red lights..."

She'd told him about the book she was just finishing, which launched them into a discussion about the talented Latin American writers whose works were finally being translated into English. He'd been so involved he'd nearly missed the turnoff to the lake. Their conversation had been a nice change, to put it mildly, from the usual talk of prime rate, teller absenteeism or something equally mundane.

Calling himself back to the present, he said, "I hope you'll like Sam, too. He's been good to me. I think he looks on me as his protegé."

He detected a shadow in her eyes, and there was an unexpected edge to her voice when she responded, "Is he grooming you for greater things?"

Matt asked quietly, "Do you think I need grooming?"

Her gaze met his for an instant, then lowered as a flush colored her cheeks. "No."

Elena knew she had to apologize. It wasn't as though she'd forgotten, even for an instant, Matt's profession. So why had she been jarred by his comment?

"Matt..." She wasn't certain what she wanted to say, and she never got a chance to find the words.

Just as Matt's expression was softening in response they were interrupted by a tall man with an angular face and snow-white hair who flung one arm around Matt's shoulder. He held out his other hand to Elena, his bright blue eyes surrounded by crinkles warm and interested. "Matt, you son of a gun, did you think you were going to get by without introducing me to this beautiful lady?"

Elena smiled and let him engulf her hand in his strong clasp as Matt interjected smoothly, "Elena, this is Sam Duncan, our host. Sam, Elena Simpson. Elena is a very talented potter."

"Is that so?"

Elena had to laugh. "If I were modest I'd disagree, but since I'm not . . ."

"No reason to be modest about something like that," he said. "Either you're good or you're not. And if you don't know there's something wrong with you."

Elena was inclined to agree, which was one reason she had never labeled Matt's air of quiet confidence as arrogance, although some might have seen him that way. As she and Sam talked, Matt excused himself for a moment to join an elderly man who had caught his eye.

Elena watched him idly, thinking how at home he was in this environment. He knew how to make his way across the room, pleasing and flattering people as he went with a smile here, a few words there, a pause to share a joke, but never letting himself be deflected from his objective. And once involved in a conversation he gave his whole attention to his partner. He wasn't guilty of the common party failing of listening to a person with only half a mind, while scanning the room for a happening that promised to be more interesting.

With a shock of embarrassment Elena realized that was exactly what she was doing right this minute. She hoped her cheeks, which suddenly felt warm, hadn't turned a betraying shade of pink. Sam would certainly wonder, since his conversation had been completely innocuous!

Just then they were joined by two other men. Sam promptly said, "Elena, meet two of my branch managers. John Peterson—" the pudgy, older man shook her hand "—and Les Thomas." The short, powerfully built black man took her hand, as well. Just as he was stepping back, Sam clapped him on the back and announced jovially, "Les here is our token black executive. Have to have one these days. Right, Les?"

Elena's eyes widened in shock at the remark; it struck her as singularly insensitive by any interpretation. Sam was laughing and had obviously intended it as a joke, but Elena didn't think people made such jokes unless at some level they meant them. And she knew all too well what it felt like to be a token employee—a woman, in her case. She still had vivid and painful memories of that experience!

When she looked at Les, she saw that he was laughing, as was John Peterson. Deliberately turning to Les with a warm smile, she asked, "What branch do you manage?"

She wasn't surprised when he told her it was Capitol Hill in Seattle. With an attitude like the bank president's, it was unlikely Les Thomas would ever have a chance to manage a branch anywhere but in a run-down, working-class neighborhood in one of the state's larger cities. If he minded that fact or Sam Duncan's remark, it didn't show on his face.

Elena hid her anger well enough to murmur an excuse so she could move away. She definitely wasn't in a mood to exchange any more lighthearted chitchat with Matt's boss. For the moment she wanted to avoid Matt, too. One part of her knew that she might be overreacting. She didn't know either Les or Sam well, and this might have been an old and well-understood joke between them. And yet Elena didn't quite believe that. For her the evening had now been unpleasantly tainted, perhaps because those few words had roused so many unwelcome memories.

She escaped to the first bedroom down the hall, thankful to find it empty. In case someone glanced in, she made a pretence of smoothing her hair in front of the mirror as she struggled to calm herself.

What had really upset her, she decided unhappily, was wondering how Matt would have reacted to Sam's little joke. She could all too easily imagine him laughing as John Peterson had and not understanding why she'd been outraged. And why should she expect otherwise? This was his world. He was one of them. It was she who was the outsider.

Well, there'd been a good reason she'd hesitated over coming tonight. She had attended enough similar parties during her abortive business career, not to mention those her parents had regularly given, to have no illusions.

Calmer now, Elena told herself again that she might well be overreacting. She'd enjoyed talking to Frances, and she liked Matt. She mustn't assume that one man's remark reflected on a whole roomful of people. Particularly, she shouldn't blame Matt for it. Nonetheless, Elena wasn't able to recapture her former mood when she returned to the party.

As she hesitated on the fringe of the crowd, idly scanning the room, her gaze locked almost immediately on Matt. He stood near the window, apparently enjoying a conversation with Les Thomas and several other men whom she hadn't met. He turned his head at that precise moment, as though he'd been keeping a watch out for her, and their eyes met. His mouth quirked into a private smile, just for her, and she felt momentarily warmed. Still, she knew her own answering smile looked as artificial as it felt. She was grateful when the crowd shifted and a man moved between them, blocking Matt from her sight before she could see his reaction.

Taking a deep breath, she pasted on an expression of pleasant interest and turned to join a nearby cluster of women, one of whom she'd met earlier. They all introduced themselves and smiled cordially, but the moment the formalities were taken care of their conversation turned back to the bank, to an avid discussion of who had been promoted and who was being transferred where. As far as Elena could tell, none of this group actually worked at the bank. Although some of them doubtless had jobs of their own, it was their husbands' careers that interested them at the moment.

She listened as one of the women said, "Did you know Hugh Watson's been made manager in Yakima?"

"No!" one of the others breathed. "Wasn't Joe in line for that?"

"Oh, well." The first shrugged with a pretense of indifference. "He didn't expect it. But Hugh! I ask you. Joe's told me stories about him. I can't imagine he'll be able to handle the responsibility."

"That's for sure," a petite, dark-haired woman agreed. "I've heard things, too. But who knows, maybe it's all for the good. By the time he bombs out, Joe'll have the seniority to be offered the promotion. Isn't your family in Yakima?"

The original speaker admitted as much. "But of course," she said, her tone reeking of insincerity, "I don't wish Hugh badly. His wife, Leila, is such a delightful person. And Joe is perfectly happy where he is."

I'll bet, Elena thought. Although, in fairness to the unknown Joe, perhaps he was, and it was only his wife who was eaten up with ambition.

As the conversation seemed to have taken a pause while the women all searched their minds for fresh tidbits of gossip, Elena grabbed the chance to ask, "Tell me, does the bank have many women in management positions?"

They all stared at her blankly for a second, before one finally said, "Oh, no. There are so few women trained for it, you know."

"No, I don't know," Elena contradicted emphatically. "I'd understood MBA programs were full of women these days."

"Oh, well, maybe," one of the group conceded. "But it takes them a while to get promoted, even though the government makes the bank give them some advantages. And, naturally, lots of women get married before they move very far up the ladder."

Trying not to sound as exasperated as she felt, Elena said reasonably, "I don't think that's true these days. Most women keep working after they've gotten married, especially ones with a career like banking."

"Well, I'm sure we'll see a change in a few years."

Elena muttered, "I certainly hope so." She might as well save her breath, she decided. None of these women cared, not as long as their husbands fulfilled their dreams. Those who had jobs obviously considered them of secondary importance, and presumably they thought that was the way it should be.

Even more depressed, Elena slipped unnoticed out of the group only to bump right into Matt, who had apparently been waiting behind her. She wondered what he'd thought of the discussion. Was this what a man such as Matt would expect of his wife?

His fingers closed firmly on her arm, claiming her. "I think we've done our duty," he murmured in her ear. "Shall we go?"

"If you're ready," she said quietly.

A long thoughtful look and brief nod from him was her answer. A moment later Matt was steering her toward the front door.

6

ELENA AND MATT walked in silence out to the car, which was parked several hundred yards down the curved lane. Although the shadows of early evening were lengthening, the sky above the ridge was still bright blue and the air was warm. Birds twittered above in the maples that lined the drive. The growl of a speedboat on the lake provided distant background noise, punctuated by the high voices of children playing just out of sight.

Those sounds were cut off once they were in the car, and the silence continued to grow until Elena's nerves prickled. She had no idea what Matt was thinking, whether he'd even guessed at her perturbation. As he maneuvered the Mercedes out of the line of parked cars and onto the main road that circled the lake, Elena sneaked a peek at him. He was looking straight ahead, frowning a little in a preoccupied way. He reached up to adjust the rearview mirror, then glanced at her with raised brows.

"Okay, Elena," he said. "Let's talk about it."

Elena eyed him warily. "What do you mean?"

"Something upset you," he said bluntly. "I'd like to know what it was."

Her smile was wry. "Am I that transparent?"

"Transparent, no." Though Matt's outward attention was on the road, Elena had no doubt he was aware of every breath she drew. "I'd say you aren't a very good actress," he went on, "and since you've been looking at me these past few minutes with about as much enthusiasm as you'd show for Frankenstein, I think I can be forgiven for wanting to know what I'm being blamed for."

Elena's cheeks flushed. "I'm not blaming you for anything," she denied. "Really! I'm just...a little sorry I agreed to come tonight. I should have known better."

Matt gave her an odd look. "Was it that bad?"

"Bad?" she repeated. "No. Just . . . not for me."

When she didn't elaborate Matt made an impatient sound, and his hands tightened on the steering wheel. He returned his attention to the road ahead. Elena, too, looked forward through the windshield.

After a minute Matt sighed. With that exhalation Elena sensed some of the tension leaving him. Quietly he said, "Why don't you give me some specifics? Tell me what bothered you."

Elena hesitated, not wanting to sound critical of his friends. Anyway, she doubted that Matt would have much sympathy for her point of view. "You'll knock down everything I say like bowling pins," she predicted ruefully.

"If I can do that, your gripes aren't worth much, are they? Shall we put them to the test?"

"With you doing the grading?" she retorted. "I think I'll skip it, if you don't mind."

Matt's voice was sharp when he retorted, "But I do mind! Damn it, Elena, if you clam up like this, how am

I supposed to understand how you feel? I don't have ESP, you know."

Elena sat silent for a moment. She didn't want to open up to him and realized she'd been resenting his insistence that she do so. But it was childish to sulk; he deserved honesty from her. "Okay," she said at last. "I'm sorry. You're right, I'm not being fair. Where shall I start?"

"Over dinner."

She was startled to find that they'd pulled up to the curb in front of McMillan's. The restaurant occupied a charming restored brick building, incongruously situated in the industrial part of Everett.

Matt got out and circled around the front of the car to open her door and help her out onto the sidewalk. Despite the tension still between them, the warm touch of his hand on hers made Elena's entire arm tingle. She stood with a jerky motion, anxious to escape the contact, only to find herself so close to his muscular frame that her breasts were brushing his chest and their thighs nearly touched. Without looking up to meet his eyes, Elena pulled quickly away, annoyed with herself. Her body wasn't cooperating with her present state of mind!

Matt pretended not to notice her momentary agitation. Elena wouldn't thank him for calling attention to what at the moment she probably considered a weakness. He followed her up the steps to the restaurant, holding open the ornately gilded door for her. The hostess showed them directly to their table.

They ordered dinner with just a glance at the menu. Both were partial to prime rib, the restaurant's specialty. Anxious to clear the air, Matt barely waited until the waitress was gone before he said, "Okay, Elena. You're on the witness stand."

She smiled ruefully. "Are you the defense attorney or the prosecutor?"

"I get the feeling," he said slowly, "that I'm the defendant. And I guess that makes you the prosecutor."

Elena stared across the table at him, her eyes wide and dark. "Don't you see, Matt? There's no right and wrong where feelings are concerned! Neither of us has to be wrong, just because we disagree about tonight."

Matt had never considered patience his strong suit and what little he had suddenly gave out. "That's interesting, coming from you," he said. "I think you've had me neatly stereotyped from the beginning, and stereotypes do imply a judgment call, don't you think?"

Elena winced but came back fighting. "No, I don't," she protested, her tone measured and reasonable. "At least, not necessarily. We all tend to categorize people we meet without even really thinking about it. Our brains are designed to do that automatically, based on experience. Most of the time the conclusions we come to are probably right, more or less, anyway. That kind of judgment doesn't have to be negative."

"No," he agreed, "it doesn't. But we're not talking in generalities. We're talking about you and me." His annoyance faded into bewilderment. "Let's not kid ourselves, Elena. The category you slotted me into is totally negative. Isn't that so?"

Elena looked helplessly at him. Finally she made a sound that might have been a laugh if it hadn't been wrenched from so deep within her. "I remember thinking that first night that you had a lot in common with

my father. That should have warned me. It did warn
me! But another part of me wanted to keep seeing you.
Even now, if you kissed me . . ." She faltered and fell silent.

A light flaring in his silver eyes, Matt demanded, "If
I kissed you, what?"

Elena's internal battle was brief. "I'd probably melt,"
she admitted bluntly, without shame. "I'd forget all the
good, sensible reasons why we don't belong together."

"Then maybe," he ventured, "all those sensible reasons deserve to be forgotten."

Oh, how she wished it was that easy! If only she
could dismiss the cocktail party from her mind, forget
what that hour had told her about Matt . . . and about
herself. She desperately wanted this evening to end with
her in his arms, as she'd dreamed it might.

"No!" She was speaking as much to herself as to him,
but Matt stiffened at her response. His eyes darkened
to the color of slate.

They were both startled by the waitress's sudden appearance. She set plates in front of them and smiled,
apparently impervious to the atmosphere.

When the woman was gone, Elena looked back at
Matt to find that his expression was carefully schooled
into impassivity. He picked up his fork and, with mad-
dening calm, took a bite of his salad. Not knowing what
else to do, Elena followed suit.

As she ate she became aware of their surroundings.
The room was dimly lit, each table wrapped in a small
golden pool of light. Other diners were leaning toward
one another, smiling, their voices low in intimate mur-

murs. The warmth Elena sensed around her just made the brittle silence between her and Matt more painful.

Matt ate most of his salad before he allowed himself to say more. He didn't begin to understand Elena's confusion where he was concerned, and he wanted to slam his fist on the table until the dishes rattled and demand answers. He'd come to know her well enough, though, to have a good idea what reaction that would provoke. His own stubbornness had more than met its match in her.

He pushed his plate away and looked steadily at her. "What happened tonight, Elena? Will you at least tell me?"

Her hesitation was only momentary. "Nothing really happened, Matt. It was just . . . small things. Those women I was talking to. All they seemed to care about was their husbands' success. They sounded exactly like my mother and her friends, only they're my generation! That scares me." He opened his mouth, but she hurried on. "I'm not saying a woman can't be happy and fulfilled sharing her husband's successes. But that needs to be truly her choice, not something she's forced into by what her husband expects. Or maybe," she added, her tone shadowed with remembered bitterness, "I should say eased into, because it happens to women without their even realizing it. They think they want to give up the chance to accomplish things on their own! After all, they're in love!" She was silent for a moment. "Well, it's important to me to have successes that are just mine. Maybe that makes me selfish, I don't know. But I guess I'm wondering if some of those women I saw tonight might not discover someday that they feel the same, and have regrets."

The waitress returned to take the salad plates and replace them with their dinners. Matt made no move to pick up his fork and knife. Not for worlds would he stop the flow now that Elena was opening up to him. He wondered, though, if it was truly those women who had upset her. Maybe she was running scared from the possibility of a deeper involvement with him because she thought that was what he would expect in a wife.

"I don't know any of those women well," he said, "but I suspect you're coming to conclusions about them a little prematurely. This was a bank cocktail party, after all. It was a natural subject for them. Probably the only thing they had in common was their husbands' careers. Who knows, maybe they all run businesses of their own on the side."

Elena's brows rose quizzically. "On the side, Matt? That's putting them in their place!"

His rueful smile acknowledged the hit. "A slip of the tongue, I promise you! Not meant the way it sounded!" It was his turn to hesitate. "Were the women all that upset you?"

"No." Her steady gray eyes met his. "There's the little matter of your boss, who seems to enjoy indulging in racial slurs."

"Racial slurs?" He stared incredulously at her. "What are you talking about?"

"Sam introduced Les Thomas as his 'token black executive.' Quote unquote. He seemed to think it was a terrific joke."

Matt frowned. "And Les?"

"He laughed, too," she admitted reluctantly.

Not altogether meaning it, Matt said, "Well, if it didn't offend Les . . ."

"Did it ever occur to you that Les might not dare tell Sam what he thinks of his little jokes?"

"No," he said. "But then, I know Sam a lot better than you do. And, I might add, so does Les."

"That's true," she conceded. "All the same, I don't think it's something to laugh about. I know what it feels like to be the token minority, and it's not a joke. It hurts. Les might not want to admit that."

"You?" Matt said in astonishment.

Elena's smile slightly cynical. "I got this terrific job with a high-class investment firm. It was a couple of months before I found out they'd only hired me because they needed a woman. They had no intention of giving me any more responsibility than they had to, much less ever promoting me. But at least I could walk away from it. That's not so easy for someone like Les."

Matt opened his mouth, then promptly closed it. He couldn't argue. Although he'd never had that particular experience himself, he wasn't so insensitive that he couldn't understand how degrading it would be.

Elena went on, "Be honest with me, Matt. Do you think Sam's joke was funny?"

"No," he admitted. "I'd say it was in poor taste. But I think you're overreacting. If Sam were a racist, Les wouldn't be the manager of one of our biggest branches."

"Which happens to be in the black district in Seattle," she reminded him.

"Les isn't our only black manager, you know. There are three or four."

Elena arched her brows. "And where are they assigned?"

Matt suddenly frowned, and in the candlelight the shadows exaggerated his expression. "What difference does it make? More to the point, what does it have to do with us?"

"Where?" she repeated stubbornly.

Matt rolled his eyes in exasperation, but obliged with a terse list. "Spokane, Everett, Tacoma . . ."

Since the towns he listed were Washington's largest, behind Seattle, and therefore the most likely to have good-sized black populations, Elena was just parting her lips to utter the unforgivable, "I told you so," when Matt added one more.

"And Walla Walla."

Elena was intimately familiar with the small, eastern Washington town of Walla Walla. She'd graduated from Whitman College, which was located there. Surrounded by rolling wheat fields, Walla Walla was a pleasant town with well-cared-for old homes, streets lined with elms, enormous lilac bushes in every yard and a citizenry that was almost entirely white. Matt couldn't have shot her down more effectively if he'd tried.

"You're sure?" she asked suspiciously.

For the first time since they'd arrived at the restaurant, his eyes held a spark of amusement. "Scout's honor."

Elena wrinkled her nose at him. "Oh, well." When Matt laughed at her tone of humorous resignation, she said more seriously, "I think we wandered from the point, anyway."

"Then what is the point?"

"That I didn't belong there tonight." She wondered why saying the truth made her feel so sad. She'd long ago chosen her life-style and was happy with it. She had no regrets. "There wasn't anything wrong with the party tonight or any of the people. I'm afraid I've sounded critical, and I don't mean to be. Sam's joke did bother me, but I know I'm extrasensitive on the subject." She shrugged. "I liked Frances and some of the other people I talked to, but they still represent a way of life and values that aren't mine. That's all."

"That's all?" he repeated, his voice tight. "Come on, Elena! How can you be so sure what they represent? We weren't there for more than an hour tonight!"

"Matt . . ." She leaned toward him, determined to make him understand. "I not only grew up in that world, I worked in it for over a year. Did I ever tell you I majored in economics in college? Then came a job in a commodity brokerage dealing in silver and gold. Naive as I was, it took me two whole weeks to discover that if they weren't committing outright fraud they were sure walking a fine line. I suppose their practices were more unethical than illegal, but it wasn't for me. So I quit."

Matt rubbed at his temple with one hand. "Elena . . . I don't see what this has to do with tonight. Or with us."

"It's . . . a question of attitude." She struggled to explain.

"Damn it, Elena!" Matt bit the words off. "There's something you're forgetting here. I am not the investment firm you worked for, or the commodity broker-age, or Sam Duncan. I'm me! Matt Terrell, remember? I'm an individual, believe it or not. I play basketball, develop my own pictures, like cats. I'm attracted to you, I have a sister I'm fond of, I wear jeans when I'm not working. That's the me that counts. Banking is nothing but my job. I went to the cocktail party to-night because it was a duty call, not because it's my idea of a terrific time."

"Ha!" she pounced. "Don't kid yourself, Matt. I saw you tonight. You loved every minute of it. You're good at it! So don't try to tell me that you don't belong, that it's not part of you."

"Then I won't," he said wearily. "What I will tell you is that it's only a small part of me, like your potting is just a fraction of what makes up the total of you. I thought we knew each other well enough that you'd be able to see that."

The pain in his voice reached Elena, and her eyes widened. "Matt, of course I do! I like you, you must know that. It's just . . . tonight reminded me what that part of your life is like. And I'm uncomfortable with it."

"That doesn't leave much for me to say, does it?" Matt sighed, and picked up his knife and fork. "Why don't we drop it for now and try to salvage our din-ners?"

Elena silently followed his example, although she wished she could have explained herself better. She'd probably sounded priggish to Matt, Little Miss Moral setting herself up in judgment on everyone else.

A moment later Matt made an inoffensive and ob-viously conciliatory remark about the weather, how it had been exceptionally good and whether that meant there would be a water shortage this summer. Elena didn't have to pretend an interest in the subject, as she got her water from a pump and it often ran dry in late summer. As they ate, conversation moved on to skiing, then other areas of mutual interest.

The atmosphere had thawed so remarkably in a short time that Elena was sorry when they'd finished their coffee and Matt paid the bill. The argument, if that was what it had been, seemed remote, so quickly had they relaxed into the light exchange.

The conversation became strained again after leaving the restaurant. As Elena had noticed before, it was far easier to suppress her physical awareness of Matt when there were lights and other people around, not to mention a table between them. Once in the car, she felt as though a bubble contained them, shutting out the rest of the world. The interior of the car seemed smaller than it did in daylight, and Matt larger. She was preternaturally conscious of his shoulder almost touching hers, of his muscular thigh just on the other side of the narrow console, of the mysteriously shadowed planes of his face. Every time he reached out to shift the gears, Elena's eyes were unwillingly drawn to his big hand, and she remembered the feather brush of his knuckles against her cheek, the solid, secure clasp on her elbow, the urgent pressure as he pulled her tight against him.

Matt, too, seemed affected by the new atmosphere and he was silent for the first several miles. Finally he cleared his throat. "How's your new bus working out?"

"Just fine," she said, relieved to have words to ward off the currents between them. "But I've hardly driven it. After all, I've only had it two days."

"I suppose it'll be a big help getting your work to shows."

"Wonderful," she agreed brightly. "I've got one coming up in just a couple of weeks, the Viking Art Show in Stanwood."

He glanced at her, and their eyes caught and held for an instant, disturbing the veneer that covered more primitive emotions. Elena was glad when Matt was forced to turn his attention to the road ahead.

She knew, with something very close to desperation, that the time had come to tell Matt that she didn't want to see him again. She couldn't afford to see him again. She enjoyed Matt's company, fervently wished to feel his lips against hers, his hands caressing as his body demanded. But she couldn't, didn't dare, forget that Matt was a banker. Elena knew all too well what that would mean to the woman in his life. She'd told him the truth tonight, and while her fears of becoming no more than an appendage might be irrational, they were real nonetheless. So if she didn't want to be hurt, she needed to make the break now, before either of them became more deeply involved.

They'd long since exited from the freeway, and the night surrounding them was even blacker now, the moon thrown into sharper relief. Elena sneaked a glance at Matt, trying to read his thoughts, but even with the car's instrument panel lit, she couldn't see his face at all. He was simply a presence beside her, the soft sound of breathing and then a muttered expletive when the car bounced into a rut.

Maybe, she thought with sudden hope, nothing needed to be said aloud. Matt was perceptive enough, and it would certainly be less awkward all around if they could wish each other a polite good night, leaving the finality of it unspoken.

By the time they reached her lighted clearing, the dogs were already in an uproar. Elena stepped quickly out of the car and crouched to their level, not caring that the hem of her fancy dress skimmed the dirt. "Daffy! Dahlia! It's just me!"

The dogs expressed a vociferous welcome, plainly calculated to make her feel guilty for having dared leave them. Elena stroked their silky heads and dodged wet tongues until their whines subsided. Looking up, she was surprised to find Matt leaning comfortably against the fender of the car, his hands thrust in his pocket. He was regarding her with a curious mixture of amusement and something she interpreted as regret.

She tilted her chin up. "Are you laughing at me?"

His brows rose in mock innocence. "Would I do that?"

Elena scarcely heard his response because, with a suddenness that chilled her like a gust of wind, she knew that she had to be honest with him. It wasn't her way to play evasive adolescent games, and she was disgusted with her cowardice in even considering taking that route.

She stood abruptly. "Matt, do you have time to come in for a cup of coffee?"

"Thank you," he said simply. "I'd like that."

He'd like it a lot less, Elena thought grimly, when he heard what she had to say. Whether he agreed with her reasoning or not, he wasn't likely to enjoy being rejected.

Elena had no sooner opened the door than the two cats greeted her clamorously, a protest as obvious as the dogs' lending a shrill note to their meows. An instant later they scooted through the opening and disappeared into the darkness.

"Ever heard of kitty doors?" Matt inquired, following her in.

"I got tired of having to rescue mice," Elena explained. She dropped her wrap in a heap on the couch before continuing into the kitchen, flipping light switches as she went.

"Rescuing . . . ?"

She glanced over her shoulder as she ran water into the bright turquoise enamel teakettle. "They like to bring mice into the house to play with. Sometimes they'd lose one behind a cupboard or under furniture, and I'd catch glimpses of it for days before I could catch it. Besides, I feel sorry for the mice. I know cats kill them, but I don't have to watch it. So I got rid of the kitty door, and I always take a good look at my cats before I let them in." She took down two of her hand-thrown mugs. "Is instant coffee all right? Or would you rather have tea?"

"Instant's fine." Matt leaned against the end of her tiled counter, watching Elena with a thoughtful expression that was slightly unnerving.

She had a feeling his mind was no more on cats and mice than hers was. Taking a deep breath and squaring her shoulders, she turned to face him.

"Matt," she began, "I've enjoyed the times we've gone out."

Matt tensed. He'd both expected and feared this and didn't know how he was going to combat it. When she paused he interjected a dry, "But... That's what you're going to say next, isn't it?"

She held his gaze, not flinching. "I guess it's obvious."

"Something is," he agreed. "Perhaps you'd better explain." He hadn't moved, but his body looked as taut as a bowstring.

At that Elena turned away and made a production of fussing with the cups and spoons. She wasn't looking at him when she next spoke. "Matt, I don't think we should see each other again."

"May I ask why?" His question was exquisitely polite.

She shifted uneasily, keeping her back to him. "You know why. We've talked about it all evening. We're attracted to each other, but our lives are so different! We want different things. All we'll do is frustrate each other if we spend any more time together."

Matt's jaw tightened. "I'm already frustrated," he said tersely, his gaze sweeping from her fragile nape down her slender back to the long legs that had first attracted him. "And I don't get it, Elena. If you were so sure you didn't want anything to do with a big bad businessman, why did you agree to have dinner with me in the first place? You don't strike me as a woman who makes a habit of vacillating."

She swung back to face him now, her head held proudly. "I'm sorry if I've frustrated you, although it must have been obvious that I didn't really want to go to that cocktail party. But you had no intention of taking no for an answer, did you? Well, maybe we both would have been better off if you had!"

At her final defiant words, Matt straightened and took a step toward her. His broad chest rose and fell with an impatient breath. It took an effort of will for him not to lay his hands on her, although whether he wanted to throttle her or kiss her he wasn't sure.

To her dismay, Elena was instantly conscious again of what a large man Matt was. It was unfair, she thought bitterly, trying to quell her involuntary physical response to his masculinity. Resisting the temptation to take a matching step back, she stood her ground and eyed him coldly, determined to hide how intimidated she felt at having him looming over her.

He responded to her speech in an annoyingly reasonable tone. "You're an adult, Elena. Okay, maybe I did push a little even though I could see your heart wasn't in it. If you'd said no and meant it, I'd have accepted your answer. But what would that have changed? I get the feeling this discussion was inevitable. If the cocktail party hadn't brought it on, something else would have."

"I think that's true," Elena agreed quietly, fighting to keep the betraying tears back. "It just goes to show that I'm right. So why don't we say goodbye without any hard feelings? We can chalk this up to experience."

Matt snorted. "All wrapped up in a neat little cliché. Tell me, was the experience good or bad?"

Elena pulled her gaze from his and stared down at the floor, her arms folded defensively across her chest. "It was . . . mixed," she muttered.

At that Matt took another quick stride toward her, and it was too later for Elena to retreat. The edge of the countertop pressed into her back; a bare inch separated her from Matt's chest. Trying to ignore the ripples of sensation his nearness provoked, she resolutely focused her eyes on the paisley pattern of his tie and took only shallow breaths.

"The water is boiling," she whispered.

If she'd hoped to divert him, she failed utterly. When she peeked upward, his eyes were fixed on her face with unwavering intensity, and his mouth had a grim set.

"Speaking of boiling . . ."

Elena tried to squeeze closer to the cupboard at her back. Perhaps foolishly, she mimicked, "You're an adult. If you can't control—"

He growled something under his breath and his hands closed tightly on her shoulders, snatching her against him. Elena gasped and squirmed to break free, but she was trapped between his hard body and the unyielding counter. As her pulse accelerated with a rush, she wondered dizzily if she even wanted to escape. She was acutely aware of the intimate feel of his strong thighs pressed against hers, of the way his chest vibrated with the force of his heartbeat under her splayed fingers. Excitement leaped unbidden through her veins, and she stilled in his grasp.

With one hand he tilted her chin up until their eyes met. His were a light, stormy gray, and she knew hers were wide with emotions she didn't want to feel, didn't want him to see.

"I don't understand you," he muttered, and then his mouth came down on hers with an insistence that was at odds with the tenderness she'd experienced from him before. And yet she didn't, couldn't, protest. Her lips parted instantly under his, and as his tongue tasted her mouth she arched against him, while with a will all their own her hands slid behind his neck. She was mindless, hungry for his touch, clinging to his strength and glorying in the feel of his hands moving urgently over her waist and the curve of her hips.

Matt had become completely lost in her sweet taste, in the heady pleasure of molding her pliant body against him. He ached to undo those tiny buttons and let her dress slip to the floor, to bury her objections in a sensual inferno. Yet somewhere inside himself he found the strength to lift his head, to release her and step back.

"Do you still want to say goodbye?" he asked roughly.

Elena stiffened. Had the kiss been calculated, then? A cold-blooded attempt on Matt's part to show her what she was throwing away? Only he hadn't emerged unscathed, either. She could see that. But still she took a deep breath and said in a ragged voice, "Goodbye, Matt."

For one moment he froze. There was incredulity and the stirrings of renewed anger in his eyes. Then, without a word, he turned abruptly on his heel and was gone.

The sound of his footsteps and the slam of the front door rang in Elena's ears. She caught a flash of headlights through the steamy kitchen window, but a moment later there was only darkness. Matt had taken her at her word, and she should be thankful. Instead she wanted to bury her head in her hands and cry. Pressing her lips tightly together to hold back the tears, Elena removed the boiling kettle from the burner and turned off the stove and the overhead light. With aching slowness she made her way to bed.

7

IN THE BLEAK DAYS that followed Elena couldn't seem to turn her mind from Matt. Weeding in her large vegetable garden, she would suddenly realize that for a good five minutes she'd been crouching in one place, the same dandelion dangling from her hand as she stared vacantly into space. Or she would be washing dishes and discover that her hands had turned to prunes in the warm soapy water while she'd been gazing out the small, paned window above the sink. Everything she did took her twice as long as it should have.

Matt's image was ever present, as though she carried a collection of snapshots in her head. The moment she wasn't occupied by something else, his face would pop up before her, sometimes smiling, sometimes guarded. The worst moments were when she pictured him angry, as she had last seen him, his eyes glittering and his mouth a taut line. And at night when she lay in bed, lost in that dreamy world between consciousness and sleep. Then she would imagine him standing beside her bed, looking down at her with the mesmerizing light of desire in his eyes, his lips softened in a sensuous curve. Sleep would slip away, leaving her wide-eyed and filled with an aching loneliness.

And yet her resolve didn't falter. She and Matt were not right for each other; the lives they'd chosen and their values were simply too far apart. It was unfortunate, she thought sadly, that they'd ever met, that by some freak of nature she responded physically to him as she hadn't responded to any man besides her ex-fiancé. No, even that wasn't true. She had been attracted to Jeff, yes, but in a pleasant, toe-tingling way, not with this searing passion.

Her potting was the only activity that seemed to capture her full attention, so she spent more and more hours at it. This was always the season she worked hardest, anyway. Her garden needed constant attention, what with weeds that grew with so much more vigor than the peas and beans and spiky corn shoots and the slugs that abandoned their normal haunts the moment the first tiny, delicious seedling appeared. On top of that, during the summer nearly every weekend was taken up by arts and crafts festivals or juried shows. She had to have an adequate inventory of work to sell unless she wanted to starve next winter.

Elena was pleased with her productivity and felt that a few of the pieces she had ready for the first shows of the season were among the best she'd ever made. One bowl in particular delighted her. Made out of the porcelain she'd been experimenting with, it flared like the open petals of a flower atop the delicate stem and pedestal. Even the glaze was perfect. The outside was done in a shimmery silver gray that did *not*, she told herself, remind her of Matt's eyes. The inside of the fluted bowl was a faintly glowing pale pink. It was one of the few pieces she'd ever created that she was almost reluctant to sell.

ON WEDNESDAY MORNING Elena was busy splitting wood when Hap and Sallie's old blue pickup came barreling down the drive, lurching from rut to rut, the rear end swiveling on the loose gravel. The moment it came into sight Elena knew who was driving.

Her friend was an unlikely daredevil, but Sallie had once confided to Elena in her soft Texas drawl that her childhood ambition had been to race stock cars. Elena wouldn't have believed that if she hadn't seen Sallie's wild driving. In her mid-thirties, Sallie Kearns was petite, with huge dark eyes and shoulder length brunette hair that naturally formed old-fashioned ringlets. Even now, as she hopped down from the high cab of the pickup, dressed in a too-large man's blue work shirt, her hair pulled back in a severe ponytail, Sallie looked fragile. Elena had discovered how deceptive that appearance was. Her friend was blunt and down-to-earth, her manner no more delicate than her driving was.

Sallie paused with her hands on her hips, smiling indulgently as her two noisy black retrievers leaped from the bed of the pickup to join Elena's dogs in an excited reunion. Then she strode over to the woodpile.

"Hard at work, I see."

Elena grimaced and blinked some sweat out of her eyes. "It's not my favorite job, I can tell you that! What's up with you? And where's Hap?"

Sallie answered, "Hap's buried in his studio making some five-foot-high monstrosity that he swears the Seattle Art Museum will take for their juried show. He even skipped breakfast." She sat down on an upended log and eyed Elena shrewdly. "I came to find out why you've sounded so evasive on the phone lately."

Elena felt her cheeks warm with a guilty flush, but with luck her face was already so red from her exertions that Sallie wouldn't notice. She put on an expression of surprise. "What on earth are you talking about? I'm sorry we haven't had a chance to get together, but you know how busy I always am in the spring. Just because you have Hap to help you with your garden . . ."

Sallie rolled her big dark eyes. "Don't try that line with me! I know you well enough to be able to tell the difference between busy and avoiding me. I figure it's explained by one of three things. Number one, I offended you. Two, you have financial problems and are afraid we'll offer charity. Or, three, man trouble. My money is on number three."

Elena made a face at her friend. "You know perfectly well that I'd tell you if you'd done something that bugged me."

"Yep," the dark-haired woman said cheerfully.

She sighed. "You never give up, do you?"

"Not this time."

Muttering a resigned, "Okay, okay," Elena propped the ax against the shed. "Let's get something cold to drink and sit on the porch. I've had enough of this for one day, anyway."

A few minutes later, glasses of cold lemonade in hand, the two women pulled their cedar chairs into the sun and settled themselves comfortably. Elena had barely taken a sip when Sallie demanded, "Well?"

She stared pensively at the trees that grew to within a few yards of the back side of the log house. "I told you about the banker I was dating."

"In passing," her friend conceded.

"Well, he really got under my skin," Elena said wryly. She told Sallie about Matt and the reasons for her decision not to see him again. "The trouble is," she finished, "I miss him. Or at least I miss what he might have meant in my life."

Sallie was frowning a little. "What's he look like?"

"Oh . . ." Without any difficulty, Elena visualized Matt. "Tall, athletic build—he played basketball for the university—blond hair, light gray eyes." She shrugged. "Terrific cheekbones. But what do his looks have to do with it?"

Her friend smiled faintly. "I wanted to know what this guy's got that all other ones you've dated don't."

"I don't know what it is about him," Elena admitted with a sigh. "Matt *is* the kind of man women notice, but it's more than that." She fumbled for an explanation. "His sense of humor appeals to me, he likes my animals, we can really talk . . . and—" honesty compelled her to add "—looking at him makes my knees get wobbly."

Sallie shook her head and pronounced, "You're in love."

Elena sniffed. "More like pure lust."

Her friend regarded her with skepticism. "If that's so, why aren't you still seeing the guy? Compatible values are definitely not required for enjoying each other's bodies!"

"I can't just go to bed with a guy I don't feel some commitment to!" Elena protested. "I'm not old-fashioned enough to expect eternal love, although that would be nice." She heard the wistful note in her voice and finished more strongly. "I wouldn't feel comfortable in a physical relationship that didn't go along with something more meaningful."

"But just think what you're missing!" Sallie pointed out, a wicked twinkle in her eyes. "Maybe it's time you loosen up a little. Anyway, who's to know?"

"Me," Elena said dryly.

Sallie looked uncertain. "Elena, are you sure that you're not in love with the guy? Because if you are, I think you might have been a little hasty. You know, you don't have to think exactly alike for a relationship to work. Take Hap and I. Do you have any idea what different backgrounds we come from? I grew up in redneck country, USA, and Hap's father teaches at Harvard while his mom gives genteel faculty teas. Let me tell you, we had a lot to work out. We still disagree about a million and one things. You've probably noticed how much more conservative my politics are than his, and sometimes he can be an incredible snob, which irritates me no end. But we love each other."

"And," Elena reminded her, "you want the same kind of life."

"That's true," Sallie agreed. "You and Matt would obviously both have some compromising to do. Maybe it's impossible. But think about it some more, okay? Because there's no such thing as a perfect man for you. Matt may put a higher value on money and position than you do, but there are probably some trade-offs. If you're lucky, he hangs up his own coat and puts the cap back on the toothpaste tube."

Elena raised her eyebrows. "Hap doesn't?"

"Never."

The conversation degenerated then into a humorous exchange on the many faults most men shared until at last Sallie drained her lemonade and decided it was time she got back to work. Elena walked her friend out to the pickup and waved goodbye, but her smile faded the minute the truck took off in a cloud of dust.

It wasn't that Sallie had said anything startling, Elena thought, anything she hadn't already considered. After all, she'd heard often enough about how compromises were necessary to make a marriage work.

Sallie had made her wonder, though, if she shouldn't have had an affair with Matt before they parted ways. Maybe the only reason she'd been on edge this past week was her unrequited desire for Matt, and she could have gotten it, and him, out of her system in just a night or two.

The thought brought a vivid picture to her mind and a blush to her cheeks. She grimaced as she turned to the house. It was too late, anyway. She couldn't exactly see herself knocking on Matt's door to inform him that she'd really like to make love to him a time or two, and *then* they could say goodbye!

Elena's depression didn't subside over the next few days. She told herself that all she needed was time. Time and keeping busy. Once she was involved in the art show the next weekend, where she'd promised to be an artist-in-action, she'd find herself thinking less about Matt.

Sunday morning Elena worked in her garden, first transplanting some leaf-lettuce seedlings she'd started in half milk cartons in her kitchen window. After lunch she went to work at her wheel, resigning herself to one of her least favorite jobs, footing.

She started by carefully centering a half-dry bowl, part of a set she'd thrown several days before. Then, bending over the spinning potter's wheel, her elbow braced to keep her hand steady, she held a tiny wire trimming tool so that it's loop just skimmed the bottom of the upside down bowl. As she gently increased the pressure, a leathery peel spiralled free, finally breaking to fall onto the tray, where it would soon be joined by other curls of the rust-red clay.

She had just picked up a wider wire tool to smooth out the track her trimming had left when her concentration was interrupted by the sound of a car engine, and the pandemonium of barking. Elena frowned. It was rare to have anybody visit or call during these afternoon hours. Her friends knew this was her favorite time to work. In fact, she usually went so far as to ignore a summons to the telephone when she was potting, but a visitor, of course, was a different matter. After only an instant's hesitation her foot left the pedal and she dropped the tool in the metal tray. As she stepped out the French door, leaving the wheel spinning in ever slower circles, she was merely curious.

She became more so when she realized that Daffy and Dahlia were no longer barking, which meant her visitor was familiar to them. She rounded the corner and stopped stock-still, her heartbeat accelerating with a frantic rush. Parked beside the shed was a charcoal-gray Mercedes.

Her incredulous gaze found the owner right beside the car, wearing a faded blue chambray work shirt and equally faded jeans. Matt was bent over, his back to her, petting the two golden retrievers.

"Matt." She uttered his name softly, with disbelief.

As quietly as she'd spoken he had apparently heard because he rose slowly and turned around, his gaze going straight to her face. Ignoring the cavorting dogs who bumped his legs, he walked toward her, his eyes not wavering from hers.

"Hello," he said, stopping a few feet from her.

Elena just looked at him. She'd pictured him so many times in the past week, and still she had forgotten how overpoweringly attractive he was. She'd thought of him as formidable, and in one sense he was. But at the moment he was almost frighteningly approachable. The way the faded denim of his jeans clung to the long muscles in his thighs, the sight of his strong brown forearms bared by the rolled-up sleeves of his shirt, made her long to touch him. And there was an appeal in his eyes that shook her, for Matt was surely more accustomed to demanding than asking for what he wanted.

And then she came to her senses, as though she'd been splashed with cold water. What *did* Matt want from her?

A whisper of a wry smile appeared on his face, and he said in a quiet voice, "Don't I even rate a hello?"

"Hello." Her response was mechanical.

"I'd like to talk to you."

Elena eyed him warily. "What about?"

"I missed you," he said softly.

His words sent a quiver of involuntary pleasure through her. "I missed you, too," she admitted.

"Then can we talk?"

"Of course we can." Doubts she might have, but she was more than ready to have them laid to rest. "Just let me cover the pot on my wheel and we'll go out back."

Matt followed her around the side of the house. "You don't look like you've been potting."

Elena had enough feminine vanity to be glad that the scene wasn't a replay of his other unexpected arrival. Although the old jeans and sleeveless, scooped-neck cotton knit shirt she wore today were far from fancy, she knew they became her, the soft fabric outlining her curves. The hours she'd spent in the garden and splitting wood had lent her normally pale skin the patina of honey, and her hair had begun to lighten as it did every summer under the sun's touch.

Matt watched without comment as she wrapped the pot in plastic to prevent its drying too rapidly, then followed her through the cool, dark house and onto the shady back deck.

"Have a seat," Elena offered politely, choosing her favorite cedar rocker.

Matt sat in the chair beside her, but leaned forward right away, his elbows on his knees. "Elena," he said abruptly, "I'd like to keep seeing you."

Matt couldn't imagine that his pronouncement would come as any surprise to Elena. She'd surely realized he wasn't a man who would give up easily. Not that he was so arrogant as to think he could have everything in life that he wanted. He simply wasn't prepared to let prejudices as intangible as gossamer stand in his way. No, in *their* way. He was willing to swear Elena had been as unhappy about their parting Friday night as he'd been.

Now Elena's tongue flicked nervously over her lips, betraying her vulnerability. "Matt, I meant everything I said that night."

"And so what? You didn't offend me. Are you afraid to have even one friend who thinks differently than you do?" Matt's voice was soft and insinuating.

Elena's fingers tightened on the arms of the chair. "That's not fair!" she protested. "You don't know any of my friends!"

"I want to be one of them," he reminded her, subtly undermining what little resolve she had left.

She gave him a steady look. "I don't think being a friend is what you have in mind."

He smiled and leaned back in his chair, regarding her with a lazy, sensuous light in his gray eyes. When he spoke, his voice was a rough caress. "Can't lovers be friends, too?"

With an effort Elena wrenched her gaze from his. "It's different."

"In a way," he agreed. "But that's not the point. I like you, Elena. Can't we be friends and enjoy each other's company even if we don't agree on everything?"

"I suppose so," she said slowly, unwilling to tell Matt what she really feared. It was one thing to have friends whose opinions and life-styles differed from hers and quite another to fall in love with a such a man.

"Elena." His voice had become warm and coaxing, and in a quick movement he reached out and clasped her hand. His touch sent prickles up her arm, akin to what she might feel if she'd been shocked by an electric current. "Elena," he said, "have dinner with me tonight. We could even go to Seattle. Maybe eat at Trattoria Mitchelli, then see what's playing at the Jazz Alley. Do you like jazz?"

Elena listened in bemusement, pleasantly seduced by the vision of a delightful evening with Matt, fine Italian food, good music, the long, delicious drive home in the dark. But then she blinked, jarred from her dream.

Of course she would enjoy it. What did that prove? Why couldn't Matt have made some effort to compromise, to find out what she might like to do and offered that instead? But, no, he wanted her to wash the dirt of her garden off her hands, accentuate her features with makeup, put on a pretty dress and become the woman he thought she should be. Every word she had said about their different life-styles had apparently fallen on deaf ears.

She knew she might regret it, but all the same she said, "Thank you, Matt, but I don't think so."

His hand tightened on hers. "Why not?" he demanded. Stubborn wasn't even the word for her, he thought in frustration. Bullheaded was more like it!

Frowning, Elena tugged to free her hand, but he wouldn't release it. "Because I don't want to!" she said childishly.

He refused to let her off the hook. They had to talk. "You can do better than that," he insisted.

Chin high, she looked defiantly at him. "I might think about it if you let go of my hand."

"Your . . ." He glanced down in surprise, then immediately freed her hand from what he realized had been a bone-crushing grip. "I'm sorry."

"It's all right," she said with dignity. All the same, he saw her surreptitiously wriggling her fingers, probably to make sure they were still operational.

He was off to a fine start, Matt thought ruefully. His colleagues at the bank would never recognize the eternally composed vice president in the man conducting this bumbling courtship. His lack of control just showed how far Elena had gotten under his skin. Which, he reminded himself, was all the more reason not to give up.

He ended the uneasy silence with a direct "Why, Elena?"

She answered honestly. "Because it's the same old thing. You want to see me, but only on your terms. I'm supposed to fit into your world. And I've told you how I feel about that."

Matt just shook his head. "Elena, I can't even pretend to understand. How am I supposed to know what fits into your world and what's in mine? I'm afraid your classification system is a little obscure to me."

A frown creased her brow. "Matt . . ."

"Never mind." He knew he wouldn't like whatever she'd been going to say, and there was only one way to head it off. "Okay, what would be an acceptable date to you? Maybe there's a local barn-raising we could take in or a corn-shucking. I'm dressed for it."

Elena stood, wishing she could laugh off his joke, but feeling too confused. "Damn it, Matt . . ."

He didn't move. "I mean it, Elena." He was completely serious. "I'm willing to try it your way. What can I do that will make you happy? How can I prove to you that I have absolutely no desire to reshape you into the image of . . . whatever you're imagining? Or is your mind so set that there's nothing I can do?"

"Okay," she tossed out. "How about this: I'd like you to give my way a whirl. Forget banking for a while. Move in with me. Help with the garden, split some wood. I'll teach you to pot. Who knows, maybe you'd discover what it's like for your life to be your own."

Matt's eyes narrowed. "Let me get this straight. You actually want me to live here, with you? Give you a chance to convert me? Is that the idea?"

Elena almost laughed aloud at his suspicious tone. "That's it," she agreed cheerfully, certain she'd made her point.

Matt's eyebrows rose and his expression became both thoughtful and slightly amused. "I think I've just been challenged."

She shrugged. "I wouldn't put it that way. You asked what you could do and I'm telling you. That's all." Of course he wouldn't be the least bit interested. He'd had one evening in mind, not . . . well, whatever she'd suggested.

A slow smile spread across his face. "Okay, you're on. I like it. Why don't we try two weeks? I'm due for some vacation, I'll take it starting tomorrow. Or is that too soon?" His last question had a mocking undertone.

"Tomorrow?" she echoed uneasily. He couldn't mean it. How had she gotten herself into a situation where he *could* mean it? And to think that she'd never considered herself impulsive. Still, maybe the experience would be good for her. Probably it *was* time she loosened up a little, as Sallie had said. Her chin lifted. "Tomorrow is fine."

Matt's smile deepened, and he rose to his feet in front of Elena so their bodies were nearly touching. Reaching out, he stroked his finger provocatively down the line of her cheek. "Tomorrow," he said in a velvet soft voice. "Leander and I will be here. We're looking forward to it."

With one last smile he turned and was gone. Elena was left frozen in place, staring blankly at the space he'd occupied, the word *tomorrow* reverberating in her mind.

8

THE EARLY HOURS of the day were not Elena's best, and one bonus of being self-employed was the fact that she could sleep as late as she chose. It was, therefore, something of a shock when she woke abruptly the next morning, her mind sharp and the pearly gray light of dawn filtering in the window. Struggling to sit up, she wondered if a sound had awakened her, but the two cats curled against her legs were regarding her with sleepy reproach. The only thing disturbing them was her.

Then she remembered. Tomorrow had come, and Matt would follow shortly. She groaned and flopped back against her pillows. Then reluctantly deciding that she wasn't going to be able to fall back asleep, Elena dragged herself out of bed and pulled on her jeans, a red chamois-cloth shirt and fuzzy knee socks. The sky outside the window was already brightening to blue, so the day would be sunny, another in the unseasonably long string of them.

As Elena sat at the kitchen table, eating a poached egg on toasted whole-wheat bread she'd baked herself, it occurred to her to wonder when Matt was coming. He hadn't said, and she'd been in too deep a state of shock to ask. Perhaps he'd have to go into the bank to request his vacation, maybe even take time to straighten out business that couldn't wait for his return. Or maybe he would simply call the bank, throw a few things in his suitcase, and appear on her doorstep by midmorning. Not knowing made her nervous.

After washing her dishes, she did a few obligatory housekeeping chores. The morning passed slowly, with Elena tensing at every distant sound. She decided not to pot, knowing that her concentration wouldn't be up to the challenge. She watered the garden while it was still in shadow, something that normally wasn't necessary until summer. After nearly a week without rain, however, the soil was dry.

A huge salad, piled with everything from bean sprouts to sunflower seeds, made up her lunch, which she ate out on the back porch in the sun. By this time she'd changed her shoes and her top, to sandals and a short-sleeved blue T-shirt with a dinosaur outlined in black on the front. Elena had scarcely finished eating when she heard the sound she'd been awaiting with mixed anticipation and dread: the purr of the Mercedes' engine.

Setting her bowl in the sink, she strolled out the front door, determined to look nonchalant. Matt was already out of the car, plucking a wire cat carrier from the back seat, and Elena abandoned her nonchalance to hurry forward. She'd forgotten he was bringing poor Leander.

"Daffy! Dahlia! Go lie down!" The dogs reluctantly obeyed.

Matt turned and nodded with a smile. "Thanks. Leander will get used to them, but it'll take a while. Maybe I should shut him in the house."

"For several days," Elena agreed, leading the way. "We don't want him to wander away. Jamaal is snoozing in there somewhere, but it's probably better if they meet on their own terms, anyway."

Elena was relieved at the casual greeting, or rather, lack of a greeting. Somehow she'd expected Matt's arrival to be more of an event, one fraught with emotional overtones. Instead they were strolling along talking about his pet as though this was an everyday visit.

Matt opened the carrier in the kitchen, carefully lifting out a sleek, blue-gray cat, who regarded Elena for a moment out of incongruously golden eyes. Springing from Matt's arms, he promptly disappeared behind the couch.

Matt inspected the fresh scratch Leander had left on his wrist. "Ungrateful beast," he muttered.

Elena couldn't help laughing.

He shot her a look of mingled irritation and amusement. "Don't I deserve a little sympathy?"

She raised her brows. "Whatever for?"

"I did get wounded in your service," he pointed out.

Elena was opening her mouth to deny this absurdity, when she suddenly remembered that he and Leander *were* here at her request. The visit had been designed to make her happy. She must have been crazy, she thought, and deliberately changed the subject. "Let's leave Leander to explore by himself. Would you like a cup of coffee or something?"

Matt's grin was teasing. "The coffee I didn't get one memorable evening?" Before Elena could respond indignantly to this pinprick, he nodded at the carrier he still held, asking, "Where shall I put this?"

"Oh, out on the sun porch, I guess."

After he'd deposited the cage beside her washing machine, Matt suggested, "What about a grand tour instead of coffee? I've never seen most of your house."

"Sure," she agreed. "Do you have a suitcase?"

The tour didn't take long; her house wasn't very big. The most difficult moment came when she led Matt up the narrow steep staircase into the loft, which at this time of day was filled with sunshine that poured in through the small-paned windows at each end and the skylight above Elena's bed. It was an oddly shaped room, high under the peak of the roof, sloping down to a height of about four feet under the eaves. The only furniture was an oak wardrobe, a beautifully carved oak dresser with a beveled mirror, a simpler oak commode that stood beside her bed and held her clock, and the bed itself—her one indulgence. Gleaming brass, it was an old-fashioned four-poster style that went well with the bright homemade quilt.

At the moment the bed seemed to dominate the room, appearing much larger than queen size, the brass posts shining like beacons. Out of the corner of her eye Elena saw that Matt, too, was looking at the bed and her cheeks warmed a little as she wondered what he was thinking. After all, his thoughts could encompass anything from an X-rated vision to simple relief that the bed looked long enough for his six-foot-three frame. For Elena it was a simple step from there to imagining what it would be like having him beside her there. Thus far she'd shared the bed only with her cats. Matt would be solid and warm, a heartbeat under her hand and soft breathing in her ear, someone to turn to and share a smile with when she awakened in the morning.

And then Matt stepped forward to set his suitcase casually down on the bed. Elena was reminded with a jolt that tonight her pleasantly exciting fantasy was going to become reality.

She took a deep breath, determined to get a grip on herself, and managed to say calmly, "I made some room in the wardrobe if you have anything you'd like to hang up."

"A few shirts," he said, sounding completely matter-of-fact. There was nothing in his expression to indicate that his thoughts had paralleled Elena's. "I left my suits at home."

"Good." Elena made for the stairs. "I'll leave you to unpack, then. The top drawer of my dresser is empty."

"Where are you going?"

"To have that cup of coffee."

"I'd appreciate one, too," Matt said. "I'll be down in just a minute."

"Fine," she agreed, not looking back as she made her escape. She definitely didn't want to watch him unpack. There was something so intimate about sharing a chest of drawers and a closet with another person. In Elena's book, you only intermingled your socks when you were ready to do the same with your lives. So why was there a man in her bedroom, unpacking his clothes into her dresser?

She sighed. This was not going to be as easy as she'd assured herself all morning it would be. She might be a grown woman, but that didn't mean she possessed the kind of poise this situation called for. Maybe she should have looked it up ahead of time in an etiquette book, she thought with wry humor.

The water wasn't even boiling before Matt made his entrance. He obviously hadn't brought an elaborate wardrobe with him. Actually, Elena had been surprised when she saw that he had only one suitcase. Although his idea of casual dress was very casual—today he wore a pair of faded Levi's and a blue plaid sport shirt with rolled-up sleeves—she'd imagined him caring more about clothes than she did.

She put a spoonful of instant coffee in each of the mugs. "Would you like to walk around the property? Or..." She stopped abruptly.

Matt had to suppress his amusement. She'd been skittish since he arrived, eyeing him with the alarm Leander probably felt for her two big dogs. What's more, Elena probably feared the same thing: that he would leap on her at any moment. Matt had no doubt of his ability to coax a physical response from her, but he wanted more, he wanted her wholehearted agreement.

"A walk sounds nice," he responded blandly. He glanced over his shoulder toward the couch. "No Leander?"

"I saw him a few minutes ago," she told him.

"Where's your cat?"

Elena smiled. "Right above you."

"Right..." Matt retreated a step and looked up. A cream-colored feline chin and two yellow paws were visible over the edge of the kitchen cupboards, and a thick ringed tail draped down the front. "Does he think he's a mountain lion?" Matt inquired. Jamaal blinked yellow-green eyes at him, apparently decided he wasn't any cause for alarm and dozed off again.

Elena laughed and poured out the coffee. "That's his favorite spot, which is fine until he decides to jump off onto a passing shoulder. So be prepared."

They carried the coffee mugs with them out into the sunshine, where they petted the dogs and made their way across the clearing to the shed. Elena opened the door and switched on the light. Just inside the door hung gardening tools, and Matt had to step around a small lawn mower, Rototiller and wheelbarrow to see the rest of the room. An old Ping-Pong table stood in the center, covered with finished pots. More pieces lined the shelves that ran along the side of the shed. A large, brick-lined kiln, which Elena opened for him, squatted in one corner.

Matt glanced around the cool, dimly lit interior. "Did you build this place, too?"

"No, it was already here," she informed him. "I think whoever put it up had it in mind as a garage. You can see the sliding doors. But then they never got around to building a house to go with it. Having the shed already here was a plus for me. It's been handy."

"Didn't you tell me once that you thought you might fix this up as a workroom?"

Elena couldn't help feeling pleased that Matt remembered something she had mentioned so casually. Encouraged by his interest, she told him her favorite daydream. "But I'm talking about a lot of money," she concluded ruefully. "By the time I insulated, put in a heating system, did something about the lighting..." She shrugged. "If we get a chance I'll show you Sallie and Hap's studio. They're my neighbors and fellow potters. They just built it last summer, and it's terrific."

Matt's eyes held hers for an electric instant. "You're talented, Elena," he said quietly. "You'll make it."

She drew a deep breath, suddenly aware of how close he was standing. The unexpected compliment combined with her reaction to his nearness shook her composure, and she instinctively stepped back.

"Thanks. Shall we go out and enjoy the sunshine?"

"Sure," he agreed obligingly, giving no indication that he'd noticed her reaction.

They left their empty mugs on the porch and began the outdoor tour. Elena felt a little silly; Matt must have guessed that she had launched into her spiel to cover her nervousness. What's more, just because she was proud of every inch of the place didn't mean he would be interested. Matt probably couldn't care less about how she'd started that row of lettuce indoors, planted that pear tree only two years ago. Nevertheless, he looked wherever she pointed and made appropriate noises.

"Transparent trees produce early apples," she told him, showing him the small orchard she'd planted. "They're not very good to eat, but they're wonderful cooking apples. Do you like apple pie?"

"One of my favorite foods," he assured her. His hands were in his pockets, and he was blinking lazily in the sunshine, looking completely at ease.

Elena continued to chatter. "I peeled and sliced some last year for the freezer, so I can make a pie in just a few minutes. I'll do that one of these days."

"Sounds good." He strolled with her along the trail that followed the tiny creek. They entered the woods, and sunlight filtered through the branches of the firs and alders. Sword ferns and high-bush huckleberries, salal, a few prickly wild blackberries and the glossy-leaved Oregon grape competed for room here under the trees, and bright splashes of color were provided by the huge yellow blooms of the skunk cabbage that thrived in the damp ground along the creek. The quiet was interrupted only by rustling bushes, parted when the dogs made forays from the path, chasing imaginary beasts.

Elena was walking in the lead, uneasily conscious of Matt so close behind. And that was absurd, she told herself. Matt was probably ambling along, admiring the woods, not thinking about her at all. He'd hadn't even looked at her today, not in a meaningful way. Even his conversation had been no more than pleasant, without a hint of provocativeness. Perhaps he was deliberately shuttering the desire he felt, trying to soothe her as he might a high-strung horse, with quiet movements and a soft voice.

Only Elena didn't feel soothed; she felt nervous. Matt's very presence made her feel pressured, as though there could be no turning back now. Not that she was at all sure she wanted to turn back. Probably this whole thing was like diving off a high board, she told herself, scary while you stood up there and made up your mind but exhilarating once you leaped into space.

"I should do some baking this afternoon," she said abruptly. "Can you occupy yourself, or . . ."

"I'm not a bad cook." His mild voice came from behind. "Lend me an apron and I'll be glad to help."

Elena couldn't resist looking over her shoulder. She tried to picture him kneading dough, a gingham apron wrapped about his tall, athletic body. Her imagination balked.

His amused expression told her he knew what she was thinking. "Don't bankers cook?" he asked.

She shrugged and turned her gaze to the trail in front. "I can't say I ever gave it any thought," she lied. "But I guess I'll find out, won't I?"

Matt's answer was a promise, delivered in a soft, sensual drawl. "There's a lot you'll find out about me in the next two weeks."

9

ELENA WATCHED MATT from across the candlelit table and her stomach quivered with a mixture of anticipation and nerves. The shifting golden flames highlighted the planes on his face, the aristocratic nose and sharp cheekbones, casting into shadow the eyes that watched her in return. Light danced off the gleaming surfaces of the gaily colored stoneware, reflected emerald prisms off the wineglasses, heightened the natural glow of the oak table.

She had made her favorite casserole tonight—chicken and mushrooms and artichoke hearts in a wine sauce—but most of the helping she had dished up for herself lay untouched on her plate. The few mouthfuls she had carefully chewed to keep up an illusion of normalcy might as well have been unsweetened oatmeal.

"Why so quiet?" Matt asked suddenly, his voice a husky caress as palpable as a hand stroking her arm.

Elena's mind went blank, leaving her without the kind of light, unrevealing answer she was determined to toss back. She could cope with Matt in the role he'd chosen to play today of the pleasant, undemanding stranger. The moment he set it aside, however, and reached out to her on a more personal level, she became rattled. And that wasn't like her.

Taking a long sip of wine to cover her silence, Elena finally shrugged. "Nothing brilliant to say, I guess."

"What?" he teased in mock astonishment. In spite of everything, his crooked smile warmed her. "I didn't think you were ever short of words!"

She retorted with pretended haughtiness, "Even I have to refuel sometimes."

Matt's brows rose and he nodded at her plate. "It doesn't look to me like you're taking in much fuel. Are you feeling all right?"

Elena hesitated. She couldn't exactly admit to Matt that her appetite for food had been taken away by an unlikely combination of melting desire for his touch and quaking nerves. Of course, it wasn't any secret between them that she was attracted to him; she'd come right out and told him so.

All the same, she had no intention of letting him discover quite how vulnerable she was to his magnetism or how uncomfortable she felt at having him here. She had to at least pretend that she was a cool, calm, collected adult, fully in control of her emotions.

After taking refuge in another sip of wine, she recovered her insouciance enough to give an impudent shrug. "I'm fine. Healthy as a horse." The wine, cool and delicate in her throat, blossomed into fire in her stomach and strengthened her wilting courage. She tilted the glass and drained the last of the wine, then set it on the table with a thump.

Matt was watching her with a speculative gaze. Strangely, she had to blink to bring his face into focus. "I think I'm getting tipsy," she observed, and a giggle escaped.

"You're not much of a drinker, are you?"

"Not usually," she agreed placidly. "But there's a time and a place for everything."

A frown creased Matt's forehead, and it seemed to Elena that his expression was suddenly wary. "What makes this the time and place for that?" he asked, nodding at the wine bottle.

She tilted her chin up. "Why shouldn't it be?"

Matt's mouth curved in a wry smile. "Let's just say I suspect your motives. I don't like the idea that you feel as though you have to escape from me."

Elena was coming to earth with a bump. "I'm not escaping, Matt," she said truthfully. Maybe that was what she'd had in mind, but she hadn't succeeded. "I'm just . . . feeling pleasant."

"You mean trying to feel pleasant. I could see how hard you were working at it. Elena . . ." He paused, his eyes searching her face. "Are you getting cold feet about this? I wouldn't be offended if you wanted me to bunk down on the couch." His grin was rueful. "Definitely disappointed, but, I promise you, not angry."

He was offering her a way out, and Elena was curiously disconcerted. Part of her had been wanting all day to believe this was a dream. Still, she hadn't been brave enough to tell Matt she had changed her mind. Now he had made it easy for her. And yet . . .

"No!" The word leaped from her, seemingly by its own power, loud and startling in the quiet, dark kitchen. "No," she repeated, steadying her voice with an effort. "That's not what I want."

And she knew then it wasn't lack of courage that had held her silent since Matt's arrival. Excitement flared in her when she looked at Matt's strong brown hands and imagined them touching her bare skin, awakening fiery sensations, when she remembered how tender his firm lips had been against hers. She needed to be held in his arms, and at this moment in her life that need was more important than her fears for the future.

Matt seemed to be waiting for something more from her. She faltered, "I just . . . I guess I am a little nervous."

"About sleeping arrangements? Or the whole thing?" His gesture appeared to encompass the long days that stretched ahead.

"I think the whole thing," she admitted, feeling a little foolish, yet relieved to have it in the open. She wasn't much good at pretense. "I've become a very independent person these past few years, and I treasure my privacy. But here I've invited you to become as intimate a part of my life as . . . oh, some old shoe tucked under the foot of my bed."

"Is that what I'm supposed to be?" There was a strong undercurrent of laughter in Matt's voice. "An old shoe?"

Elena had to smile, too. She had never met anyone who fit that description less than Matt Terrell. Even now, dressed in the same faded jeans and open-necked sport shirt he'd worn this afternoon, his elbows propped on the table and the set of his shoulders relaxed, Matt had an air of assurance, a vibrancy, that would make him stand out in any crowd. It was impossible to imagine him scuffed or slumping or defeated by life.

Matt's gaze was intent now, although his tone was light when he spoke. "Do you often bring old shoes home?"

Elena actually chuckled. Did he need to ask, after spending the day watching her shy at every shadow? "What do you think?" she challenged humorously.

Matt answered frankly, "You've looked scared to death since I got here. I'd think you had never brought a man home with you, except you have too much poise to be completely inexperienced. And I know it's none of my business," he added wryly, before she could open her mouth. "So don't get on your high horse."

He wasn't usually interested in a woman's past loves. His curiosity had been piqued from the beginning, though, by the contradictions that made up Elena. He'd guessed that her nervousness today was rooted in more than virginal shyness; she'd responded too whole-heartedly to his kisses to be afraid of physical intimacy. And yet he couldn't be sure. He found himself wanting to know.

Color was warming Elena's cheeks, and her gaze had dropped from his as she traced one finger over the smooth rim of her plate.

"I guess I've made it your business," she admitted in a low voice. "And, no, I've never brought an old shoe home before, you're right about that. Once upon a time there was a fancy new one, though." She looked up and gave an odd smile. "I was engaged a few years ago. It was while I was still Daddy's little girl, obligingly majoring in business." Elena's eyes were focused on Matt, but he knew it was the past she was seeing now. "Jeff was most women's dream." Her voice became brittle.

"Handsome, successful, ambitious..." She stopped speaking, leaving them staring at each other, newly sprung tension stretching the moment out.

At last Matt said flatly, "And you think I'm like him."

"Aren't you?" The words were out before Elena could stop them.

His brows had drawn together, giving his face a forbidding aspect. This, she thought distantly, was the Matt Terrell who could foreclose on a helpless creditor, fire an incompetent employee, make decisions that earned money for the bank but hurt people.

"Is it a sin to be successful, to want to do your job well?"

Elena could almost feel the sparks arcing between them, filling the air with an electric charge that made her skin prickle and her hands tighten into fists. "It is if you sacrifice everything else in life that's worthwhile." She pressed her trembling lips together. "And most ambitious people do."

Matt began rubbing at the back of his neck with one hand, trying to release his frustration, but anger was a cold knot inside him. Elena persisted in seeing him through blinders and he was beginning to wonder if it was hopeless.

When he spoke it was with sarcasm that was unusual for him. "Don't you think that's a slight overgeneralization? Or have you been taking polls? 'Excuse me, sir, does your wife or your job come first?'"

"That's not fair!" she cried.

"Are you being fair?" He couldn't back down, not now.

Her teeth sank into her full lower lip and her gray eyes shimmered with a rush of tears. "No," she said in a stifled voice. "No, I'm not. You're right. I'm sorry."

There was a long, aching silence, and then he said softly, "Was he such a bastard?"

"No." She looked almost startled by her own reply. "He was considerate, loving, everything I could want, except . . ." She sighed. "I wasn't really a person to him. Just a wonderful new possession, like a house or a car. He thought my potting would make a nice hobby once we were married, but of course I was going to be kept busy entertaining. I was a charming hostess, according to him, and he was a lucky man to have me to show off. Naturally I wouldn't need a career." She grimaced. "I think Jeff was an escapee from the nineteen fifties. Just the kind of man who inspired women's liberation, although he was cleverly disguised. Actually, I'm probably making him sound worse than he was, but I could see him trying to turn me into a woman just like his mother. Dependent, in other words. And I had the feeling that if he got a business call in the middle of our honeymoon, the call would be more important than me."

"Do you really think I'm like that?" Matt asked with genuine curiosity.

Elena's pulse quickened with anxiety and she closed her eyes, shutting out the sight of his lean, quizzical face. "I don't know," she almost whispered. "I don't think so, but . . . There's something about you that makes me afraid."

After a moment's silence she forced herself to lift her bowed head and open her eyes, not knowing what to expect from him. Unfortunately, his expression told her little; his jaw muscles were set, and the line of his mouth was hard and straight, but if he'd been angry he no longer was. Instead, he appeared merely determined.

After a moment he said evenly, "Elena, this visit was your idea. You shouldn't have invited me if you're so sure I'm nothing but a clone of this other man. I think you owe me a chance."

He was demanding, not asking. Elena's breath came faster between parted lips. She couldn't have looked away from him if she had tried. The ice gray of his eyes seemed to have melted into his pupils. She was staring at deep pools, silver from the moon glinting off the surface, their centers black, swirling whirlpools.

He reached across the table to her, holding out his hand with compelling certainty. Her trust instinctive, she laid her hand in his. The room was suddenly warm, the darkness soft and velvety; it enclosed them like a cocoon. She moved her hand in his to return his clasp, feeling with pleasure the texture of his skin against her palm. With his thumb he began tracing patterns on the inside of her wrist, sending delicious sensations up her arm.

Elena let her eyes move from the planes of his cheeks to the softness of his gently smiling mouth. His gaze lingered on her lips, too, and on her slender shoulders, the curve of her breasts . . . They were just a man and a woman, differences in life and philosophy put aside for one night.

Matt stood and tugged at her hand, and Elena let herself be pulled to her feet into the haven of his arms.

She lifted her mouth eagerly to meet his warm, searching lips.

When Matt raised his head and spoke, his voice was husky, "Let's leave this, shall we?" He nodded toward the table.

Warmed by a tiny spark of mischief, Elena gave a provocative smile. "We have to have dessert."

The molten glow in his eyes brightened. "I intend to," he murmured, turning her firmly in his arms and leading her toward the stairs.

Anticipation tightened her stomach as they silently climbed the steps into the moonlit loft. Faint silver light from the huge windows at the end gave the room an unearthly feel. It was like a secret cavern in a crystal-clear sea. The moonlight and shadows intermingled and shifted as the evening breeze stirred the tips of the Douglas firs outside.

By unspoken consent Elena and Matt both looked out at the dark field below them and the nearly full moon hovering just above the trees. Elena saw a pale shape slip by the black silhouette of the shed, and she knew one of her dogs was out for a walk. The scene was so familiar, but because Matt was beside her, it seemed touched by a magical brush. She turned toward him.

Sliding one hand under her fall of silky hair, Matt caressed the back of her neck; his fingers became entwined in her hair. With gentle pressure he urged her closer, and she began to sway toward him—irresistibly drawn, as she had been from the moment they met.

Her lips were parted when he bent to kiss her, and the slow trickle of warmth within her became a rushing flood. Their mouths met with impatient hunger, and whatever invisible walls had divided them crumbled completely. Matt lowered her to the bed and she pulled him down with her. She was frantic for the feel of him, and her hands moved under his shirt, kneading and stroking with a will all their own.

The uncertain voices in Elena's head had long since stilled, and she was conscious only of the pressure of Matt's body against hers and the soft give of the bed under her back. His mouth left hers to trail across her cheek, nibble at her earlobe, lay a string of kisses like white-hot pearls around her neck, then return with increased urgency to her waiting lips. One of his hands cradled the back of her head, while the other traced the line of her waist and hip, the curve of her breast.

He began to undress her, undoing each button of her cotton blouse slowly and deliberately, letting his fingers linger against the silk of her skin. When he had freed her from the delicate lace of her bra, he cupped her breasts in his palms, drawing feather-light circles around her nipples with his thumbs. He smiled with pleasure when she shivered and arched toward him, reaching out to fumble with the buttons on his shirt with impatient fingers.

As Elena ran her hands down Matt's chest she reveled in the feel of the soft springing hair and the sleek muscles that tightened at her touch. She heard him murmur, "You're beautiful," his voice so rough it was unrecognizable, but tonight everything about the way he touched and communicated was unrecognizable, from the gentleness, so unexpected in a man accustomed to command, to his obvious vulnerability.

His mouth found hers again, coaxing, demanding, until the languorous passion of a moment before was swallowed again by a fierce urgency. Their clothes were gone, their bare legs entangled, and the weight of Matt's body pressed her down into the quilted softness. His tongue probed, heightening her excitement, and his hands moved unceasingly over her body, gently stroking, teasing.

When he parted her thighs, she dissolved, melted into his body. They came together and she cried out, her fierce pleasure almost painful. She lifted her hips to meet Matt's thrusts in a response so elemental it was beyond thought. She clutched at him with sweaty palms, buried her face in his throat, while her senses spiraled. She felt the tremor that shook Matt at the same time as the honey-sweet, exquisite wave swept over her.

They lay together for a long while, not talking, just holding each other close. The tenderness between them was tangible.

The whisper of Matt's breath brushed her temple, and Elena pressed tiny kisses against his neck. Right now, she thought fleetingly, they were close, as close as two people could be.

10

ELENA AWOKE the next morning lying in her usual position, curled up on her side and facing the windows. Sunlight was warm on her face, and she blinked sleepily, watching tiny motes of dust dance on the faint air currents. She felt deliciously content and decided it must have something to do with the heavy arm draped across her waist and the warm body pressed against her back. Smiling dreamily, she snuggled closer.

At her tiny movement Matt's muscles tightened, and the next instant his lips were softly touching the back of her neck. "Good morning," he whispered. "At last."

"Umm," she murmured in return, pushing her hips back against him. "Morning."

Matt smiled at the throaty sound of her voice. His hand moved, tracing indecipherable patterns on her stomach and brushing the fullness of her breasts until she squirmed against him. "Rat," she muttered, grabbing his wrist and placing his hand firmly over her breast.

He chuckled, delighting in her ready response to his touch. As his fingers closed on her taut nipple, he savored the texture of her breast, the soft curve and hard nub. He let his fingers slide sensuously through the silky mass of honey-brown hair that tangled across the pillow, then bent over her to plant kisses down her spine.

"I thought you'd never wake up," he murmured. "I've been waiting." His hand moved to her thigh, his fingernails grazing her skin ever so gently.

Elena tensed until she was trembling and thought she might explode if she couldn't touch him in turn. In a sudden movement she flipped over in his arms, so her body was pressed against him and her mouth was inches from his lips.

"Good morning," she repeated, her voice deliberately sultry, her smile slow. She moved her hips invitingly and slid her bare foot up and down his strong calf, enjoying the feel of springing hair and hard muscles.

The lazy triumph in Matt's gray eyes was instantly replaced by a hot light. His arms closed fiercely around her and his mouth took hers with a passionate hunger. She had the hazy thought that this was how loving was meant to be and wasn't even startled at her own choice of words.

They came together with a wrench of nearly unbearable pleasure, their urgency as great as it had been the first time. Afterward they lay in each other's arms, completely, breathlessly still. Slowly Elena again became aware of the sunshine and all the usual morning sounds. The clock on the commode ticked patiently. Jamaal was stretched languorously on the floor. Everything around her was so utterly normal, so far removed from the astonishing passion she and Matt had just shared.

Her head rested on Matt's shoulder, and she felt his heartbeat slowing, his breathing resuming its slow, even pattern. She wished she knew what he was thinking, or that she dared ask. She hadn't known lovemaking could be like this. But, of course, she was relatively inexperienced. Maybe for Matt it was different. Somehow that thought was unwelcome, and she shied away from it.

When Matt spoke his chest vibrated under Elena's ear. "That didn't happen quite the way I planned it."

She lifted her head a little so she could see his face. "What do you mean?" she asked carefully.

He smiled faintly. "I lay here while you were sleeping, and I imagined how I was going to make love to you. It was going to be slow and sweet. I wanted to touch and taste every inch of your body. Only then," he sounded rueful, "I lost my head."

Now she dared. "It's not . . . usually like that?"

He heard the uncertainty in her voice and reached up with his free hand to run his fingers down her cheek. "Never," he said, surprising himself with the intensity of his tone. "I've never wanted a woman the way I do you. It's one reason I've become so frustrated on a couple of occasions. I couldn't believe, with the sparks flying between us the way they were, that you were just telling me to go home and forget it."

Elena rested her head on his shoulder again, loving the warmth of his skin under her cheek. "It wasn't easy," she said. "I was . . . torn."

"I could tell," he responded dryly. He smoothed her long straight hair back from her face now, curling the thick strands around his fingers.

"I didn't think physical desire was enough," Elena told him, knowing she sounded priggish. "I still don't," she felt compelled to add, not caring how much that statement might betray.

Matt lifted his head from the pillow to look at her with mock indignation. "Are you trying to tell me my body is all you like? You don't enjoy my scintillating conversation?"

"Well . . ." She pretended to think.

The next thing Elena knew, she was flat on her back, and Matt was tickling her sides. She giggled and squirmed, pushing ineffectually at his chest. "You rat!" she managed.

His big hands stilled, and the laughter in his eyes was transformed into something quite different. "The last time you said that," he murmured, "I wasn't tickling you. It seems to me—" his hand moved to cup her breast while his thumb gently teased the nipple "—that I was doing something like this."

Elena looked helplessly up into his glittering eyes. "I believe you were," she agreed, her voice light and breathless.

"Do you still think I'm a rat?" His mouth hovered above hers.

"Of course," she murmured almost inaudibly. She reached up to run her fingers through his soft hair.

This time he did explore her body with exquisite attention to detail, and she did the same to him. When they came together at last it was slow and sweet, just as he had promised.

His weight was heavy on her as they rested, but Elena loved it. She didn't want him to ever move. She thought if they could lie here forever in the aftermath of such earthshaking pleasure, in the warmth of the sunlight and the tranquility of the morning, their hearts beating in tempo, that she could be happy. But then, she reminded herself, she'd thought the same an hour ago. In truth, the storm was far too exciting to want to stay in the peaceful eye of it for long.

Finally Matt did move. But instead of remaining lazily beside her, he sprang out of bed.

"Time's awasting!" he announced, pulling open the dresser drawer. "Are you going to teach me to pot or not!"

Elena groaned and pretended to cover her face with the pillow. "Are you always this cheerful in the morning?"

He glanced at her in surprise. "Morning? I hate to break it to you, Elena, but it's ten o'clock. Practically lunchtime."

She pulled the pillow aside to glare at him. "Ten o'clock," she informed him in dulcet tones, "is still morning."

"Anyway," he said, having already collected his clothes, "we've been awake for hours. So what are you grumbling about? You should be bursting with energy."

"I used it all up." She grinned and clambered out of the high bed.

After a delightful shared shower, Elena dressed in a pair of soft corduroy jeans and another of the T-shirts she liked to wear, this one depicting three wolves howling at the moon. Matt glanced at it and shook his head, smiling.

Elena was relieved when he declined her offer to fix him a substantial breakfast. She wasn't fond of overloading on eggs, toast and hash browns so early in the day, but she'd figured that, as Matt was a guest, she should make some effort to defer to his normal habits. He seemed perfectly happy to pour himself a bowl of cereal and slice a banana on top.

"What do you do for exercise?" she asked, coffee cup halfway to her mouth.

He regarded her with amusement. "Are you trying to tell me that I need some?"

She chuckled. "No, just the opposite." She let her eyes rove over his smoothly muscled body. "It just occurred to me that you couldn't have a build like that if you didn't do anything but sit behind your desk."

"I run," he told her. "And play basketball."

"Who with?"

"I belong to a couple of city league teams. One in Seattle and one right in Everett, at Paine Field. And sometimes I just play in pickup games."

"You said you played at the university," she recalled. "Were you actually a starter?"

"A starter?" he repeated indignantly, sitting up straighter. "I was All-Pac Ten. I was a star!"

Elena plunged her spoon back into her cereal bowl. "No kidding," she said mildly.

Matt grinned. "You're rough on a man's ego," he complained. "You were supposed to swoon at my feet."

"Is that what your ego depends on?" she inquired with interest.

His grin became rueful. "No. But it probably did at one time."

Elena pushed her bowl away and propped her elbows on the table. "You were really good, huh?" she asked, more seriously this time.

"I was good," he stated matter-of-factly. He took a sip of his coffee and smiled. "But I wasn't Magic Johnson."

"Were you a guard?"

"No, a forward. Which is one reason I didn't go on to the pros. I'm only six-three, so most likely I would have had to adapt to being a guard, and, frankly, I wasn't quick enough." He shrugged.

"But if you were that successful as a college player..." she protested.

"Oh, I could have made the team. I was drafted by Detroit," he remarked as an aside. "But I'd have probably ended up sitting the bench, and that's not what I wanted. If I couldn't be the best, I didn't want to do it at all."

"Do I detect some sour grapes?" Elena teased.

Matt laughed, but answered seriously, "I don't think so. The thing is I had an alternative, unlike a lot of players. I finished my degree in four years and my grades were high enough to get me into a top graduate school. So..." He spread his hands in a gesture of finality.

Elena stood and carried her bowl and cup to the sink. "Well, let's see if you have any artistic talent, shall we?"

They went out to the sun porch, where she supplied Matt with a rubberized apron. She showed him how to knead clay to get rid of air pockets, then demonstrated centering a piece on the wheel. Using her sponge she squeezed water over the clay, making it slippery under her hands.

"This is the hardest part," she told him. "Once you get the knack of centering, you have it made." She hesitated, then amended with a crooked smile, "Well, almost. Most beginners make the walls of their pots too thick, and it's another breakthrough when your pieces have genuinely interesting shapes."

Elena watched as Matt worked at centering a glob of clay. His elbows were braced, but he was allowing the clay to move his hands instead of imposing his will on it. She smiled a little as she saw the frown of concentration on his face, much the same look he had when giving his attention to something at the bank.

His expression didn't change when he said casually, "By the way, does your objection to going to dinner the other night extend to all outside entertainment? Because I have tickets tonight to—"

Elena had been sitting on the shelf behind her wheel, about to make a helpful suggestion to aid Matt's thus far inept efforts. At his words she interrupted, "We can't go anywhere tonight. The Lakers are playing!"

He looked up and grinned. "You mean Seattle's playing."

She passed it off. "Same thing."

Matt lifted his hands from the clay and leaned back with an air of satisfaction. "As I was saying . . . I have tickets for tonight's play-off game at the coliseum. So if you want to root for the Lakers, here's your big chance."

"Now that," Elena said happily, "is the kind of date I can't turn down. You're on!"

THEY ENDED UP having dinner at Jake O'Shaughnessey's, only a block from the Seattle Center. The restaurant specialized in salmon broiled over an alder fire, but

Elena managed to find room for a dish of their delicious homemade ice cream, as well. Afterward Matt and she strolled toward the coliseum, enjoying the early evening.

The center was dominated by the silhouette of the space needle, built for the 1962 World's Fair. Matt glanced up at the glass-fronted elevator carrying people to the observation deck or perhaps to dine in the restaurant. Elena's gaze followed his.

"I haven't been up in it since I was a kid," she said, her head tilted back and her eyes narrowed against the bright sky.

"Shall we go up?" Matt asked.

Her eyes widened in astonishment. "Are you kidding? I hate heights. You couldn't pay me enough to get me in that elevator!"

Matt held back his laughter. "The view is sensational," he pointed out with a straight face. "Just think, tonight we'd be able to see the Olympics and the Cascades. Even Mount Rainier is clear."

Elena wrinkled her nose. "Thanks, but no thanks."

Matt reached out and gathered Elena to his side. "Do you know," he murmured huskily in her ear, "I almost wish we were home."

She slipped her arm around his waist and slanted a provocative smile up at him. "Almost?"

"Well..." His smile was mischievous. "I'm very fond of basketball. And this is the play-offs."

"Boy!" Elena exclaimed with pretended indignation. "What a romantic!"

Matt grinned. "I look at it this way. We can go to the game now, and home later. Contrary to the old saying, I can have my cake and eat it, too."

She shook her head and laughed. "I know I should be grossly offended. But since it's the Lakers playing . . ."

"Somehow I thought you might forgive me," he said dryly.

Their seats were in an ideal location, at nearly center court and in the fifteenth row. The two teams were already warming up, and Elena watched with fascination. Although she followed the sport assiduously, most often she listened to games on the radio or occasionally saw one on television at a friend's house. Neither electronic medium could convey the sense of immediacy she felt at actually being here or bring to life the color and excitement.

The game started with a bang, although not one that pleased the crowd. The Los Angeles Lakers were famous for their explosive, breakaway offense, and tonight the team played like a well-oiled machine, jumping off to a six-point lead. Elena didn't feel the slightest bit inhibited by being one of only a handful of Lakers fans in the audience; she was on her feet lustily cheering whenever her team made a basket.

She'd expected Matt to watch the game with that air of dignified cool he so often employed in public. She'd wondered if he would be embarrassed by her vocal support of the Lakers. She discovered quickly that Matt took basketball much too seriously to be a detached observer. The first time the referee blew his whistle on the Sonics, Matt erupted to his feet.

"Offensive foul! Is he crazy?" Still grumbling along with the rest of the crowd, he finally resumed his seat. Elena didn't say a word, but he cast her a sour look. "I can feel that smile," he accused.

She let him see it. "Yep."

Elena and Matt alternately yelled at their teams and groaned in despair as the score seesawed. Elena was enjoying Matt's company immensely, but caught up as she was in the spirit of rivalry she wouldn't have admitted it for the world. It was fun to watch the game with someone who shared her enthusiasm, and she appreciated his superior knowledge. He pointed out weaknesses and strengths in both teams that she would never have noticed and saw trends developing long before they were obvious.

To the delight of the crowd, the Sonics began to pull away with two minutes to go, and the Lakers didn't respond. The game was over even before the final buzzer sounded.

As Elena and Matt joined the delirious crowd filing out, she remarked grumpily, "We are still up two to one in the series, you know."

Matt's reply was cheerful. "After tomorrow night it'll be all tied up, you just wait and see."

"Maybe," she allowed. "But then they go back to Los Angeles."

Matt shrugged. "Just for one game," he reminded her.

Their amicable argument lasted until they came to the center's fountain, lit by night in a jeweled array of colors. They paused to admire the rainbow mist, and Matt put his arm around Elena's shoulders, pulling her close to his side. After a minute he said softly in her ear, "Who cares about basketball, anyway?"

Elena's nerve endings were reacting to Matt's nearness, and the heat of his body was warming her along the length of their contact. The entire subject of basketball faded in importance.

"I'm willing to put aside our differences," she murmured.

"Good." He turned her slowly to him, and his free hand slid over her hip, caressing at the same time as he pressed her intimately against him. Their gazes clung as he bent his head, and then his lips met hers. They kissed, wrapped in a velvety languor, their mouths gentle and their tongues tasting, touching, teasing. There was no demand, no urgency, yet the kiss was wildly sensuous.

At last, Matt lifted his head. "I think," he said raggedly, "it's time we went home."

THE NEXT WEEK was a time of delightful discovery for Elena. Matt was a far more complex man than she'd imagined, and each day brought fresh surprises.

One hobby that he shared with her from the beginning was his photography. He'd brought his cameras, and he explained patiently how the light meter worked, taught her about F-stops and how to balance the shutter opening with the camera speed. He took pictures constantly. Pictures of her pulling weeds in the garden, a swath of dark earth brushed carelessly across her cheek, of Marigold lolling in the wheelbarrow, of a bobbing flower against the weathered gray of the shed. Elena was intrigued by the compositions he chose. If she'd been visiting someone, Instamatic in hand, she would probably have taken a stiffly posed portrait and maybe a shot of the house from well back. Her creative conceptions were formed in clay, his in the more ephemeral medium that recorded light and shadow and color.

Elena also confirmed that Matt was a perfectionist, with a very low tolerance for any kind of incompetence. He was doing well for a complete beginner at using the wheel, but he didn't see it that way. Instead, he was annoyed with himself for the failures that were a normal part of learning to throw. Matt wasn't impressed when Elena pointed out that he probably couldn't play basketball like Kareem Abdul Jabbar the first time he'd picked up a ball, either.

One night he took her to watch him play basketball with a summer city league. She expected a casual game played for fun in an atmosphere of camaraderie. But from the moment the men, dressed in a motley assortment of sweats, shorts and T-shirts, circled for the jump-off it became obvious that they took their sport very seriously.

Elena was one of a small group of women sitting on the folding wooden bleachers. Several of them had small children; others were dressed as though they'd come straight from work. They seemed to know each other well and chatted throughout the game, never taking their eyes off the court. And Elena could see why. Although she had known she would enjoy seeing Matt in action, the game was played with such fervor that it gripped her attention. The men leaped and collided, coming down from rebounds with elbows swinging, shouted encouragement and insults to each other as they ran down the court, and generally played with an intensity that wouldn't have been out of place in the NBA championship game.

Matt's team won the game, partly thanks to his twenty-eight points, and she could see by his complacent expression how pleased he was as he wiped sweat off his face with an old towel. He pulled on baggy gray sweats over his shorts and thin basketball jersey, talking excitedly all the while with his teammates.

On the way out to the car Elena couldn't help teasing him.

"Feeling good?"

"You bet!" he said cheerfully. "There's nothing like winning."

"Nothing?" she echoed with amused emphasis.

He grinned jubilantly at her. "Nothing! Not to say—" he slipped a hand under the crook of her elbow "—that there aren't other equal pleasures."

Elena just laughed. "I think you're reliving the good old days."

Matt gave some serious thought to that. "No, I don't think so. We wouldn't enjoy it if that's what we were doing. Because in some ways the game is frustrating for ex-college and pro players like most of us are. None of us are in the shape we once were, so we have to enjoy what we *can* do, and not think about the way we would have done it once upon a time."

"I hadn't thought about it that way," Elena admitted. "I suppose you have lost some of your skill." She'd been impressed enough with Matt's speed and grace on the court, with the way his long body extended as his hands flicked out to drop the ball unerringly through the hoop. She hadn't considered that he must once have been better still.

"Some?" he grumbled good-humoredly. "Too much! I'm getting old, you know. I'll have to give up the game pretty soon. Can't play it from a rocking chair." His sidelong smile kept her from taking him very seriously.

"I CAN'T DRIBBLE," Elena explained nervously, clutching the basketball in both hands. "It always wants to bounce off my foot or my knee."

"It wants?"

"Well, you know what I mean."

He grinned. "Yeah, I do know. Sort of."

The day was another unseasonably warm one, and they were standing in the middle of the outdoor basketball court behind the local middle school. Matt had decided, to Elena's consternation, that she should learn to play.

"Really," Matt said, his gaze moving over her in an entirely new brand of assessment, "you shouldn't have any trouble. You're tall enough, you have long legs, I haven't seen any signs of you tripping over your own feet . . ."

Elena wrinkled her nose at Matt. "You're making me feel like a steer that you're thinking of butchering!"

"Anyway," he said, taking the ball from her, "you wouldn't want to admit you're too old to learn a new game, now would you?"

"Certainly not," she agreed solemnly. "So let's get this show on the road. I'm not getting any younger, you know."

"Let's start with shooting," he said. "We'll put the dreaded dribbling off until another day."

"I'm no hotshot at scoring points, either," she confessed.

"But you have a master for a teacher," he pointed out. Elena might have felt compelled to remark on a certain lack of modesty inherent in this claim, but he chose that moment to spin away, casually bounce the ball between his legs, twirl, then shoot it over her head. Naturally, it slipped through the net with barely a rattle.

"Take that," he said.

"Is that nice?" she reproved mildly. "How am I supposed to block your shot when you haven't taught me how yet?"

"That's one lesson we'll never get to." Matt's cocky grin brought forth Elena's laughter. "Even I'm not that good a teacher!" In a couple of long strides he recovered the ball, then tossed it to her. "Catch."

He waved her to a place on the court that was right beneath the basket, then watched as she awkwardly heaved the ball up. It missed the metal hoop by a mile. She wondered how, in Matt's hands, this same ball appeared feather-light, a graceful extension of his fingers.

"All right." He caught the ball and came to stand very close beside her. "First of all, you need to bend your knees, even hop a little. There's a reason it's called a jump shot, you know. You're not strong enough to just throw it up without getting your weight behind it. And then you need to shoot it with one hand. The other one's just for support. See?" His long body uncoiled, and his hands flicked out. As naturally as a bird in flight, the ball rose in a smooth arc and dropped through the hoop, then bounced back toward him. He tapped it in her direction. "You try it."

It took at least ten attempts before the ball actually rattled through the hoop. Elena beamed at Matt, feeling absurdly proud of her achievement. "I did it! Did you see? It went in!"

"I saw." His gray eyes glinted with amusement. "Your technique is looking better, too."

"Is it?" Elena pursed her lips and bent her knees, staring with intense concentration up at the basket. She

The more you love romance . . . the more you'll love this offer

FREE!

Mail this heart today! (see inside)

Join us on a Harlequin Honeymoon
and we'll give you
4 free books
A free makeup mirror and brush kit
And a free mystery gift

IT'S A
HARLEQUIN HONEYMOON—
A SWEETHEART
OF A FREE OFFER!
HERE'S WHAT YOU GET:

1. **Four New Harlequin Temptation Novels—FREE!**
   Take a Harlequin Honeymoon with your four exciting
   romances—yours FREE from Harlequin Reader Service. Each of
   these hot-off-the-press novels brings you the passion and tenderness of today's greatest love stories...your free passports to bright
   new worlds of love and foreign adventure.

2. **A Lighted Makeup Mirror and Brush
   Kit—FREE!**
   This lighted makeup mirror and brush kit al-
   lows plenty of light for those quick touch-ups.
   It operates on two easy-to-replace batteries and
   bulbs (batteries not included). It holds everything you need for a perfect finished look yet is
   small enough to slip into your purse or pocket—
   4-⅛" x 3" closed.

3. **An Exciting Mystery Bonus—FREE!**
   You'll be thrilled with this surprise gift. It will be the source of
   many compliments, as well as a useful and attractive addition to
   your home.

4. **Money-Saving Home Delivery!**
   Join Harlequin Reader Service and enjoy the convenience of pre-
   viewing four new books every month delivered right to your home.
   Each book is yours for only $1.99—26¢ less per book than what
   you pay in stores. And there is no extra charge for postage and
   handling. Great savings plus total convenience add up to a sweet-
   heart of a deal for you!

5. **Free Newsletter**
   It's *heart to heart*, the indispensable insider's look at our most
   popular writers, upcoming books, even recipes from your favorite authors.

6. **More Surprise Gifts**
   Because our home subscribers are our most valued readers, we'll
   be sending you additional free gifts from time to time—as a token
   of our appreciation.

START YOUR HARLEQUIN HONEYMOON TODAY—JUST
COMPLETE, DETACH AND MAIL YOUR FREE-OFFER CARD

Get your fabulous gifts
ABSOLUTELY FREE!

MAIL THIS CARD TODAY.

PLACE
HEART STICKER
HERE

GIVE YOUR HEART
TO HARLEQUIN

YES! Please send me my four Harlequin Temptation novels FREE, along with my free lighted makeup mirror and brush kit and free mystery gift as explained on the opposite page.

NAME _____
(PLEASE PRINT)

ADDRESS _____ APT. ____

CITY _____ STATE _____

ZIP CODE _____

142 CIX MDMV

PRICES SUBJECT TO CHANGE. OFFER LIMITED TO ONE PER HOUSEHOLD AND NOT VALID TO PRESENT SUBSCRIBERS.

HARLEQUIN READER SERVICE "NO RISK" GUARANTEE

— There's no obligation to buy—and the free books and gifts remain yours to keep.
— You pay the lowest price possible and receive books before they appear in stores.
— You may end your subscription anytime—just write and let us know.

PRINTED IN U.S.A.

START YOUR
HARLEQUIN HONEYMOON TODAY.
JUST COMPLETE, DETACH AND MAIL YOUR
FREE OFFER CARD.

If offer card below is missing, write to: Harlequin Reader Service, 901 Fuhrmann Blvd.
P.O. Box 1394, Buffalo, NY, 14240-1394

jumped again and, as her arms extended, the ball slid off her fingertips. Her hand even flipped at the wrist, just as Matt's always did, and the ball went neatly through the rim. "Hey!"

She tried it from the other side, then from farther away. Most of her shots still sprang off the metal rim, but at least they were doing that much. Until now, when she'd thrown the ball up it generally touched nothing but air.

She and Matt started taking turns, running after each other's vagrant shots, which meant Matt did most of the running. And that was just as well, Elena decided. She needed to catch her breath, a problem Matt didn't seem to have. Besides, she enjoyed watching him in motion.

Elena had been amazed at the condition of the clothes Matt chose to play in until he informed her with apparent seriousness that a smart basketball player always stuck with something that was comfortable.

"Comfortable?" she'd repeated doubtfully, eyeing the huge hole in the knee of his sweatpants. "Is that what it is?" And then a slow triumphant smile spread across her face. "Aha! I've got it! You're superstitious! You figure you won't win if you throw those ratty old pants in the rag bag!"

Matt's eyes hadn't quite meet hers. "A good friend gave me these."

"Maybe he'd give you some new ones."

"It wouldn't be the same," he said stubbornly.

"Do you let the phases of the moon tell you when to invest money, too?"

Matt had laughed. "Nah, I save all my good luck for basketball games. They're more important."

He had on a thin white T-shirt today, with the faded purple letters UW on the back. The shirt was streaked with sweat and clung to the supple muscles in his back and chest, giving Elena a splendid opportunity to admire his physique. He loped up to her with the ball, smiling at her. His eyes were narrowed against the bright sun, but his thoughts were easy enough to read.

"Anybody ever tell you sweat is sexy?" he asked, his gaze moving sensuously over the thin red jersey that dampness had molded to Elena's curves.

She let her eyes caress him with similar intent. "The thought had occurred to me. Just now, as a matter of fact."

Matt tucked the ball under one arm and grasped her elbow with his free hand. "I think we've accomplished enough for one lesson," he said, steering her purposefully toward the parking lot that lay to one side of the brick school. "I'm ready to move on to . . . another activity."

"You have a one-track mind," she teased, but her feet weren't hesitant in keeping up with his.

"Not at all," he assured her. "Only when I look at you."

"Is that a compliment?" she asked, her lips curving.

"Absolutely! Would you want it any other way?"

"No." Elena hadn't had to give that much consideration, not when the simple touch of his hand on her arm sent shivers of expectation through her.

Matt's smile held unmistakable satisfaction. "We'll come back tomorrow."

THE DAYS that followed continued to be spiced by the passion that underlay their every look and touch. They made love at night, in the moon-streaked darkness, and again in the golden light of morning. And sometimes even that wasn't enough.

One sunny afternoon Matt and Elena were picnicking by the creek. They had decided to eat outside on impulse and the menu wasn't elaborate; just cheese and fruit and some rolls Elena had baked. Not bothering to spread a blanket, they just sat in the tangled, yellow-green grass. Where they settled on the bank of the tiny stream the grass crushed under their weight, forming a natural nest for them that shut out the rest of the world.

After she and Matt finished eating, Elena sat cross-legged, dreamily watching the sparkles dance across the clear, shallow water. Matt, who wore only a pair of dark blue running shorts, lay back in the grass, his hands clasped under his head. His eyes were closed and he seemed to be dozing in the sun's warmth.

His short hair gleamed like pale gold, and in contrast his skin was tanned a warm brown. Elena's eyes lingered on his long torso, on the smooth muscles and the gilding of hair on his chest, the flat plane of his stomach just above the shorts, the brush of gold hair under his arms. The taut lines of his face were relaxed, and he looked very vulnerable.

Without even thinking she reached over and put her hand on his chest. Matt didn't move nor open his eyes, but she felt his awareness, the instant tension at her touch. She smoothed her hand over his warm skin, the soft hair tickling her palm, then down his hard stomach, at last slipping her fingers boldly under the band of his shorts. He lay still and Elena smiled as she lowered her mouth to follow the path her hand had blazed. She liked the salty taste of his skin, the heat where it had absorbed the sun's rays, the satiny texture and the steel of the muscles that lay beneath. Her kisses trailed to his waistband and back up again. She nipped gently at his neck and rubbed her cheek against his, enjoying the slight abrasiveness.

When Elena pulled back slightly to look at Matt, it was to find his face a heart-stopping study in contrasts. His eyes, open now, were a molten silver, heated by the passion her touch had awakened. His lips, though, had a loving curve that weakened her even more than did his desire. When he held out his arms in silent invitation, she tumbled unhesitatingly into them.

He rolled over until Elena lay on her back in the grass, his broad shoulders silhouetted above her. With his index finger he softly traced her parted lips, the line of her cheek and down her neck to the hollow at its base. His concentration was so complete, his touch so delicate, that he might have been a blind man seeing her in the only way he could.

Elena reached up to frame his face with her hands and a smile trembled on her lips. She was melting inside, Matt's gaze filling her horizons. Suddenly he was smiling, too, his intensity transformed into a warmth and tenderness that filled her heart with joy, so easily might it have been love. When he bent down to touch his lips to hers both were still smiling, and Elena felt the sweetness.

Matt slowly lowered the straps of her thin cotton shirt, rolling it to her waist, while Elena noted distantly how white her breasts were against his brown skin. That difference—her paleness, his darkness, her soft fullness so close to his hard strength—made her long for more closeness yet.

He pressed his mouth to her throat, then kissed the curve of her breast. "You're so lovely," he murmured as he lifted his head. Elena wanted to tell him that he was, too, but she was afraid he wouldn't understand that she really meant it; words so often made light of deep emotions. So instead she just smiled again and let her hands speak for her.

They parted only as long as it took to slip off their shorts, then Matt entered her with a slow deliberate stroke. Her legs tangled with his as she willingly followed his lead in this most elemental of dances. Pleasure exquisite in its intensity unfurled within her and filled her with joy until at the very last she had to cry out, lost in his embrace.

"We're probably both permanently marked with grass stains," Matt remarked, taking his weight off her. "Especially you."

Elena made a face. "Now I know why you were so eager to be on top."

He spread his hands in a gesture of innocence. "You didn't think it was because of my masculine ego, did you?"

Elena laughed and leaned forward to kiss him lightly on the mouth. "How could I ever suspect you of having too big an ego?" she mocked lovingly.

They continued to banter as they dressed and gathered up the scraps from their lunch. Elena was unkind enough to remind Matt about the basketball game they'd listened to on the radio the night before. The Lakers had finished the Sonics off and were to meet Houston in the semifinals of the NBA play-offs.

"I wish I wasn't doing that artist-in-action thing tomorrow," she said suddenly.

Normally Elena enjoyed the rare occasions when she could demonstrate her work for interested people who were browsing a show. She couldn't help being gratified, as well, by the chance to sell more than the three pieces she'd entered in the show, and without having to pay a commission. That was one of the privileges an artist-in-action earned. The days of Matt's stay seemed to be passing so quickly, however, that she was reluctant to lose one of them to an activity that didn't include him.

"Don't worry about it," Matt said, and she could tell by his voice he knew what she was thinking. "I'm looking forward to seeing the art. I can entertain myself in town. And if I get bored," he said, grinning, "maybe I can give you a break and show off my potting technique to the multitudes. At least it's original!"

THE NEXT MORNING Matt helped Elena carry her wheel out to the VW bus and they loaded it in the back, along with a box of tools and the selection of stoneware she intended to try to sell. She'd delivered the pieces that were entered in the show earlier in the week.

Elena drove, conscious of Matt beside her, watching. Driving was one of the things Elena did just a little sloppily. She tended to roll through stop signs if no cars were coming, not wanting to have to shift into first, and she'd gotten a couple of tickets for not yielding the right of way. She knew herself well enough to suspect that if she had a fast car, speeding would most likely be added to her sins. It wasn't that she liked to drive fast or ever deliberately broke the law; her mind just had a habit of wandering to something more interesting than what was happening on the road.

Today that subject was Matt. Elena was anxious for him to be impressed by the show, especially because the one jarring note in their idyllic days had been his attitude toward how she ran her pottery business.

At first she'd been pleased and even flattered by his interest. Over dinner one night she had explained how she sold her work.

"I have three basic outlets. I sell some at shows, the bulk at galleries and fairs. In one way the fairs are best because usually you just pay a set fee to have a booth, not a percentage. What sells there is usually the lower-priced stuff, though—plant pots or toothbrush holders, sometimes mugs or bowls. People browsing at fairs don't buy the more expensive pieces or whole sets of dishes. Those things do well in galleries, but the owners take such a big cut of my profit—thirty to forty percent—that I have to mark up the price. I hate to do that, and I still make less than I would if I sold the same pot at a fair."

Matt was frowning. "Can't you wholesale your work? At least then you'd know exactly what you were going to need and could apportion your time accordingly."

"There are places I could wholesale," Elena admitted. "But I've never wanted to. If you get into that market you just become a machine, making the same things over and over. I consider myself a production potter, but with the emphasis on potter. I don't want to throw the exact same pot week in and week out, finishing it off with the exact same glaze. And that's what a retail outlet of that sort wants. If a particular pot does well, they expect you to keep turning out the same design."

"But couldn't you produce pottery faster if you repeated the same form a number of times?"

"Sure," she said tartly. "I could also bore myself to death."

"A certain amount of boredom is a part of almost all jobs," Matt pointed out with what she interpreted as impatience. "It seems foolish to settle for a substandard income when you could do better with a little streamlining."

"Streamlining?" she repeated in horror. "What you're suggesting isn't streamlining. It's a change of profession."

They had left the discussion there, but it hadn't been the last. Matt was bothered by Elena's lack of a system in her workroom. He couldn't understand why she didn't have a regular schedule for each step of the creation process.

"You mean I should always glaze on Thursdays and fire on Fridays? Is that what you're suggesting?" she asked.

The stark disbelief in her voice apparently got through because Matt glanced up from the cylinder he was throwing on the wheel and answered, "Not necessarily those specific days, but that's the idea. If nothing else, that would set an automatic quota for you. The way you're working now—firing whenever you have enough done to fill the kiln—makes it easy for you to be lazy. And you've told me yourself that you run out of inventory during the summer."

Elena shook her head in amazement. "You sound like my grandmother. She washed on Monday, ironed on Tuesday, baked on Wednesday... Regular as clockwork for her entire life. I like to think we've become emancipated from a schedule like that."

"Housewives have been," Matt agreed, "but not everybody has. Most businesses work that way, you know. They might make up orders one day, bill the next, call customers." He shrugged. "You're running a business here and that should mean striving for a certain amount of efficiency."

"I *am* efficient!" Elena retorted defiantly, trying not to look around at the clutter. She kept her glazes in what could only be described as haphazard order on one shelf, and unfortunately, Matt had seen her search fruitlessly through the jars more than once. Twenty-five pound bags of clay were everywhere, plaster bats were piled wherever space allowed, newly glazed pots were mixed with greenware on the shelves, and tools and brushes were dropped wherever she'd finished with them.

Matt was gentleman enough not to look around, either. His mouth quirked with amusement, though, as he diplomatically returned his attention to the spinning wheel.

Elena was more bothered by these discussions than their substance actually warranted. In fact, normally she might have appreciated them; Matt had a different perspective than hers, and she knew she could learn from him. Under the circumstances, however, all such talk did was remind her of a side of Matt she'd have rather forgotten. She was doing her best to live his stay as though it was a dream with no past and no future. The last thing she wanted was to be reminded of the unpleasant reality that separated them.

It was important to Elena that Matt should enjoy this show and respect at least this end of her business. If he was expecting something fancy, however, he was in for a shock. The Viking Art Show was held at the Sons of

Norway Hall in Stanwood, which was a small farming community. The hall was basically one large room with a bare wood floor. The atmosphere was reminiscent of a barn, which wasn't altogether inappropriate for displaying art. Her pottery, for example, showed up strikingly against rough wood. Partly for that reason the pieces she'd chosen to enter were stoneware rather than the more delicate porcelain she'd been working with lately.

Content to be quiet, Matt had enjoyed watching the changing expressions on Elena's face as she drove. He couldn't help wondering what so preoccupied her. Was she nervous about potting in front of spectators? Or was it the reception her work would receive that worried her? Her art was very personal, and it must hurt when people turned away without interest or with a disparaging remark, or when nothing sold.

As Elena was turning the VW off the freeway, he broke the silence with an open-ended comment. "Your big season is just getting started."

"Mmm," she agreed, accelerating onto the side road with an exuberance that made him wince. She was impervious to his reaction. "Most of the big arts and crafts festivals are outdoors," she explained, "which means summertime. They're not the prestige places to show, but they're where I sell my largest volume. I make more in a weekend when I take a booth at, say, the Edmonds fair than I do in a month during the winter. See," she added with a glint of humor, "I'm not quite as unbusinesslike as you think I am."

Matt ignored her last comment. "What do you mean by prestige?" he asked. He was finding the art world, with its eccentricities and customs, fascinating. Elena's business was quite different than any other he'd encountered.

"The juried shows," she told him. "The best artists concentrate on selling a few exceptional pieces for appropriately high prices. I know some potters who would sneer at the idea of turning out dozens of plant pots to sell in a booth the way I do."

"Then why do you do it?"

The highway stretched arrow-straight ahead of them, and Elena's gaze remained on it as she answered with revealing honesty, "A couple of reasons, I guess. One is that I really enjoy people. Having a booth at a fair is fun. I like talking to browsers and I like having something to sell them that they can afford. I'd miss all that if I were more of an elitist. And then there's the brutal fact that I'm a good potter, but not one of the very best. Sometimes I do well in the smaller juried shows, but I can't compete at the top level. Of course, I've only been at it a few years, so I hope I'll get better. But sometimes I think I just don't have that extra flare." Her eyes met Matt's momentarily. "Too pedestrian a nature, I guess."

Matt regarded her profile thoughtfully. "Does that bother you?" he asked after a moment.

"You mean not having that extra something?" At his nod, she smiled. "No. I enjoy what I do, and I'm satisfied with how I do it."

He'd already discovered that much, he thought wryly. In fact, she was stubbornly resistant to the idea of doing things more efficiently. Which probably meant that she thought it would lead to greater evils—such as acquisitiveness—to be avoided at all costs.

Elena's cheeks were suddenly touched with pink as she realized her comment might have sounded like a slap at him for his criticisms. She hurried on, "I work at improving, but we all have different special qualities. If outstanding creativity just doesn't happen to be one of mine, well—" she shrugged with elaborate and, he suspected, false indifference "—that's the way it is."

Matt frowned a little. "You underrate yourself."

She didn't hesitate. "I don't think so."

There was no chance for him to carry the argument further as they had arrived. She backed the bus up to the front door of the wooden building. It took them only a few minutes to unload, after which he parked the VW in back while Elena began setting up with the help of a couple of women working on the show.

She was glad to see a fair number of people wandering through the maze of dividers that held the paintings and even more happy to discover the sold stickers on two of the three large pieces of stoneware she had entered. The pottery and wood carvings were displayed at the ends of each row, and Elena was pleased with the arrangements. They'd used packing crates draped with hand-loomed hangings, and the combination of textures was very effective.

She chatted with the man who had taken the morning stint as artist-in-action, a watercolorist whose work she admired. He had been to the patron's party the night before and told her that was when her work had sold.

"I think the same couple bought both pieces. I heard somebody tell them you were going to be here today, so don't be surprised if they show up."

"Maybe they'll order a twenty-piece service," she said hopefully. "To go with their new casserole."

He laughed, and she asked the obligatory question: "How's your work selling?"

The painter grimaced. "It's not. I think I've priced myself out of this market."

"Well, don't complain." Elena stood back and tilted her head as she studied the display of stoneware she'd set out. "Just because you're a hotshot now . . ."

"Is that why I'm going to the Dairy Queen for lunch instead of the Blue Griffin?" he asked mournfully over his shoulder.

Elena wrapped a voluminous apron around her waist, unpacked some clay and got to work. As usual a cluster of people gathered to watch as she deftly centered the clay and smoothly pulled it up into a cylinder. She heard one woman mutter, "That takes me an hour!" and smiled. There were a million amateur potters out there, and they all envied her the expertise that allowed her to be a professional. But she'd learned just as they had, only she'd stuck to it longer.

The more difficult part was turning the clay cylinder into a shape that would be functional as well as aesthetically satisfying. The curve had to be just right, the lip of the pot neither too thick nor too delicate. The height had to be in balance with the width of the flare. Today she experimented with interesting forms because she was creating purely for the enjoyment of her audience. As she finished each pot, she squished the clay into a clump and placed it in a plastic bag. Wet pottery was impossible to transport; the motion of the car was sure to shift it off balance if it didn't sag out of shape altogether.

She answered questions as she worked. Many were very basic, but others were more technical—concerning the use of slips in decoration, how she'd achieved particular effects with glazes, how different types of clay determined her techniques. She also sold a number of the pieces she had brought.

All the while she was conscious of Matt moving slowly through the maze of dividers, studying the paintings and sculpture. She was almost relieved when he at last emerged on the far side of the room, gave her a casual wave and disappeared out the front door. He had a most distracting effect on her. Now she could concentrate more fully on her wheel work and her audience.

Her thoughts refused to cooperate, however. She found herself thinking about the conversation they'd had in the car when he had told her she underrated herself. What had he meant by that? He could be such a paradox, she thought, complimenting her with every appearance of sincerity one moment, criticizing her methods the next. His comments about her production would seem to indicate that he thought she was just a hack whose only hope of making a real living was cranking out pots for a wholesaler. And yet he'd made reference to her talent several times.

In a way, that Matt had bothered to criticize her business practices at all could be considered a compliment of sorts. At least it showed that he was taking her seriously.

Her reflections were interrupted by a question, and from that point on she stayed busy enough to keep her mind off Matt. She was surprised to be told several hours later that it was four o'clock, time for her to pack up and go home. With just a glance around she could see that the show had been a success; small red "sold" stickers abounded. It had been a success for her, too, she decided with pleasure. Despite her initial reluctance and her preoccupation with Matt, she had enjoyed the afternoon. And, unlike sometimes, she had something special to look forward to at home that night.

"WHAT DID YOU THINK of the show?" Elena asked eagerly, as she maneuvered the VW bus out of the gravel parking lot.

Matt's response was noncommittal. "It was interesting."

"Interesting?" she repeated, disappointed. "What do you mean by that?"

His brows arched. "Just what I said. I've been to art shows before, but never thought about it from the artist's perspective. Today I did." There was a short pause. "Tell me," he said, "are the pictures hung in any sort of order?"

Elena glanced at him in surprise. "Of course. Although it varies, depending on who does it. Today—"

she had to think for a minute "—it was color. All the pastels were together."

"Color?" He was incredulous. "What's the sense in that?"

"Hanging the paintings so they display to the best advantage is an art unto itself," she explained patiently. "You don't want a painting to be completely overshadowed by those around it, and you ought to be able to look at a whole cluster of paintings and not be jarred by any one. A delicate portrait of a child done in chalk, say, wouldn't hang well next to a powerful, vibrant seascape. So sometimes colors are used to categorize. Other shows I've been to have used theme. That's interesting because you can compare how different artists have handled essentially the same subject."

Matt was frowning. "But what if you've come looking for a particular artist's work? Wouldn't you expect them to be hung together?"

"That can be a problem," Elena admitted. "Of course, the bigger shows have catalogs."

"It wouldn't cost much to put one together even for a show this size."

She shrugged. "People don't complain."

Matt was becoming exasperated by her blithe attitude toward the more nitty-gritty realities of business. He couldn't resist pointing out a harsh truth: "But they also may not buy. I saw a landscape, for example, that I liked very much. But if I was going to spend six hundred dollars on a painting, I'd want to know whether the artist just had a good day when he painted that one or whether he was genuinely talented and his work was likely to appreciate in value. I glanced around, but without conducting a major search I couldn't find any others by him. So I didn't buy.

"Do you see what I'm saying? It seemed to me there were a number of things that could have been done to make this show more profitable. I'd have started with a big sign outside. I presume there was advertising, but why not try to grab people who might stop by on impulse, as well?"

He knew he'd pressed too hard the moment he saw her expression. And then she said with unmistakable frustration, "Do you ever think about anything except how to make more of a profit?"

He wondered with sudden bitterness if that was really how he appeared to her. In as controlled a voice as he could manage, he said, "You of all people should know I do."

Assailed by a flash of memories—laughing, tender, passionate—Elena was silenced. It was a minute before she was able to say quietly, "Yes. I'm sorry. But I don't understand how you could have studied those paintings for an hour and all you can think to say about them is how they could have been displayed so they'd sell better. Can't you see that they're more than just merchandise?"

"I didn't mean to imply otherwise," he said. "I simply see no reason why artists can't also be businesslike. Why starve in a garret if, with a little extra work, you can live in reasonable prosperity?"

There was nothing in his tone now to indicate that he'd been hurt by her words, and Elena continued the discussion on the impersonal level he'd placed it. "I don't think artists are by nature good businesspeople," she said. "Maybe it's the right brain/left brain thing."

Matt shrugged. "I don't believe anyone is that strongly dominated by one side or the other. Anyway, I'm not suggesting a course in accounting practices. The techniques I'm talking about could be learned and implemented by anyone."

"Even Slop-along Simpson herself?" Elena asked with a sudden flash of humor.

His mouth twitched. "I was making a general observation."

The next several miles passed in silence, but Elena felt herself weakening. Curiosity killed the cat, she reminded herself, but still she was unable to resist.

"Okay, tell me about these simple-as-pie techniques."

Matt just smiled enigmatically. "I think you've heard more than enough of my suggestions."

"Matt . . ." Elena hesitated, then said carefully, "I'm really not as closed to new ideas as I'm afraid I've sounded. I'd like to make a better income if I could do it without sacrificing my artistic integrity." She hoped that didn't sound pompous. "It's just. . .the way you go about it that bugs me. You analyze everything to death. Can't you ever just enjoy?"

His gray eyes glinted. "What you don't seem to realize," he said, "is that analyzing something and enjoying it aren't mutually exclusive. We humans are amazing creatures. We can actually do two things at once. In this case, the fact that I'm analyzing why a painting I admire hasn't sold doesn't mean I can't also be moved by it."

"But why is it," she challenged, "that the only part you ever talk about is the analyzing?"

Matt was taken aback by her question. There was more than a grain of truth in it. "I suppose," he mused, "because it's concrete. How do you put into words the feeling a particular scene rendered with a particular brush stroke gives you? And don't try to tell me about that gobbledygook art reviewers write."

Elena chuckled. "I wouldn't dream of it! I don't read that junk. And I must admit you have a point. But, you know, I didn't expect much. I would have been perfectly happy if you'd just told me you liked so-and-so's paintings. At least then I would have known we were on the same wavelength."

"I think I could manage that much," Matt said gravely. "I didn't know you were so easy to please! I liked Jack Dorsey's paintings, especially the one of the tide flats. Also Wes Broughton and someone who did watercolors, mostly of children. Pale, clear colors."

"Oh, Carol Seppala! I love hers, too. If I had a child I'd have Carol do a portrait."

Matt's thoughts were suddenly diverted by the vision of Elena as a mother. Her child would have her fine bones and soft light hair. And big gray eyes that lit up with every smile. Elena would make a good mother. He wondered if she was ready to have children, and how she would feel about having them with him.

Something must have showed on his face because Elena was looking at him in a puzzled way. With an effort Matt pulled his mind back to the present. "Those ceramic sculptures were interesting, too."

Elena's expression brightened and she smiled. "The monster and his minions? Those were Hap's. You know, the neighbor I keep mentioning. He's one of those potters I told you about who wouldn't dream of taking a booth at the fair. Of course, he doesn't have to. He's very talented."

"Does his work sell well?" Matt asked, genuinely curious. "I don't think I'd want a monster in my living room."

"His work sells very well. And for prices that make me blink. But I know what you mean. It would scare the wits out of me to turn around suddenly and find one of those things staring at me. Speaking of Hap," she went on, "Sallie would really like us to come over for dinner. I told her no last week, but . . ."

"I don't mind," Matt assured her. "Even if we both know what she really wants is to look me over."

Elena stole a peek at him. There was amusement in his eyes, and he was smiling tenderly.

"I'd like to meet your friends."

THEY HAD the next two blissful days to themselves. Elena demonstrated glazing techniques to Matt, getting a fair number of pots ready for their second firing in the process. She at last made the apple pie she'd been promising him, and they spent several hours at the never-ending task of weeding the garden.

The weather had turned rainy, but Matt and Elena simply spent more time potting, or they read lying on the rug in front of the Franklin stove—it was the first time in nearly a month she'd built a fire. They talked for hours, sharing memories of their growing-up years. They played cards; one night it was a delicious game of strip poker that ended with a predictable storm of passion.

If Elena felt anything lacking, she hid it even from herself, refusing to ruin this last week by worrying about the future. Come Sunday there would be time enough for that. All the same, she became increasingly aware of the moments when it would have been natural to say, "I love you," and they both stayed silent.

On Tuesday night they set out to have dinner with Hap and Sallie. Driving over in Matt's Mercedes, Elena smiled to herself thinking what Sallie would do if she ever got behind the wheel.

Her friends' house had started its life as a log cabin about the size of Elena's. Over the years, though, various owners had tacked on clapboard additions. Despite the lack of planning, the house was charming. Elena was particularly fond of the enormous fireplace fashioned from rounded rocks taken from the nearby streambed. Hap had installed several wood stoves in other rooms, but even in the interests of heat efficiency he hadn't been able to bring himself to block up the fireplace with an insert.

Matt's eyebrows rose as he surveyed the house; they rose even higher when Sallie met them at the door.

Without a trace of inhibition she surveyed him and pronounced, "You're every bit as sexy as I'd expected."

"Thank you," he said, with what Elena thought was admirable aplomb. He surely wasn't used to such bluntness. "I take it Elena gave me a strong advance billing."

"Oh, Elena." Sallie waved her hand dismissively. "I judge by what she *doesn't* say. She's too closemouthed for her own good."

"My kind of woman," he agreed pleasantly.

Sallie placed her hands on her hips. "Have I just been insulted?"

Matt grinned, obviously enjoying the dialogue. "Not at all. I don't know you that well, do I?"

"Well, in that case..." Sallie smiled broadly and stepped aside. "Come in, come in. We're having lasagna. I hope you don't mind. Hap got it in his head to cook, and that's his one and only recipe. He likes to show off. Visitors go away thinking he's a gourmet cook and that I'm lucky to have him. If only they knew!"

Hap's initial attitude toward Matt was much warier than Sallie's. He came out of the kitchen looking his usual disheveled self in faded jeans and shirt, his dark beard and wavy hair in such disarray his features were mostly hidden. He wore an incongruous red and white gingham apron tied around his waist.

He and Matt shook hands. Hap nodded. "Good to meet you."

"It's a pleasure to meet you," Matt returned. "I wanted to tell you how much I admire the sculpture you had on display in the Viking Art Show. All three pieces were remarkable."

Hap's reserve began to melt. "I *was* pleased with the way the monster came out," he admitted. "Cracking can be a real problem with multisection forms, and that was the largest one I've tried. And the crackle effect..." He looked slightly sheepish. "Sorry. I don't suppose you're interested in technical difficulties."

"Actually, I am," Matt corrected. "That is, insofar as I understand them. Elena's been teaching me to throw." He smiled at her with unmistakable warmth. "I'm already an expert on some technical difficulties. Like clay sagging."

Hap and Sallie both laughed. "Everyone who's tried potting has had that problem!" Hap said. "But, hey, I'd better get back to my lasagna."

"Can I help?" Matt asked.

Hap looked surprised at the offer, but shook his head. "I just have to carry everything out."

As they ate, talking between mouthfuls, Elena couldn't help contrasting Matt with her two friends. She hadn't expected him to fit in with them as well as he did. But she could tell that Sallie liked his easy comebacks and forthrightness, and Hap responded to the intensity in Matt's voice as he talked about his photography. Maybe Matt wasn't as different from her friends as she'd imagined, Elena reflected.

Just then something Hap said caught her attention. She tuned back into the conversation to find that they were talking about the Viking Art Show.

"It's a small one," Hap commented. "But well run. What did you think, Matt?"

Matt hesitated for just an instant, his gaze resting on Elena. Her expression was both amused and encouraging, and he knew her well enough now to be confident that she would expect him to be honest.

"I thought they could have done more to attract people," he said. "Their advance advertising must have been adequate, or they wouldn't have gotten the crowd they had, but a big sign out on the street wouldn't have hurt. I noticed a lot of traffic passing and some of those people might have stopped if they'd known there was an art show going on."

Sallie was nodding. "You're right."

Elena interjected blandly, but with a spark of humor in her eyes, "Matt has been nagging me about promotion and production. He insists that we local artists don't push ourselves hard enough."

Matt cocked an eyebrow. "Are you playing the devil's advocate, here?"

She made a face at him, but the tinge of pink on her cheeks told him that was exactly what she'd been trying to do.

Matt smiled. "I don't know enough about how Hap and Sallie run their business to offer any criticism."

"Oh, we'd be interested in any suggestions you have to make." Hap insisted. "Business isn't our strong suit."

"Well . . ." Matt demurred, then he grinned. "I don't want to be coy, so here goes. One thing I wondered is why none of you have business cards. Or do you?"

Elena's friends silently shook their heads, and of course he knew the answer where she was concerned.

"They cost very little to have made up," he said. "And I think they really pay off. When Elena was the artist-in-action, for example, dozens of people stopped to watch her, ask questions or buy her work. If she'd offered each a card, they would have had her name and address available later, say if they decided to buy a gift for someone. And she's told me that a good part of her business consists of making entire sets of dishes for customers. Well, that's not the kind of thing people are likely to buy on impulse, which is where the card comes in. Somebody who sees her work and likes it can go home and think about it, then give her a call. The way she's operating now, they probably don't even know her name. If she's going to depend on custom work, she should make sure people know where to find her."

Elena wasn't sure how she felt about being his case study, but had to admit there was truth in what he'd said. In fact, she couldn't imagine why she'd never thought of business cards herself. She had certainly come from a background where they were proffered as quickly as a handshake, and some artists did use them, she supposed. To her, business cards had always seemed to go with suits and ties and briefcases, not clay and jeans.

"Another thing," Matt continued. "Why not keep a mailing list? If somebody is especially interested in your work, add them to your list. It would be worth the postage to let all those people know where you're showing at any given time. There would be some initial expense, but again, I think it would pay. The psychology is important here. I think people would be flattered that you considered them important enough to notify.

"And for you, Hap—more than for Elena or Sallie—calls to special customers might be in order. Your pieces are more highly priced and idiosyncratic so your pool of potential buyers is smaller."

Hap nodded, looking thoughtful.

"Well, if you knew who your buyers were, you could call. Ask them to a special viewing." Matt grinned. "I'll bet they'd fall all over themselves to come."

"I don't know about the calls," Hap said dubiously. "I'd have a hard time being that aggressive selling myself. But your other idea sounds good to me."

"Another thing." Matt was leaning forward, his face alive with enthusiasm. "It seems to me that your biggest problem is the cut the middleman takes out of your profits."

This time he was answered with three vigorous nods. The forty percent gallery owners took always rankled.

"Elena told me once she thought her place was too isolated for her to sell directly from there. I can see, too, that her production isn't high enough. What I'm thinking is that a group of you could get together and have a kiln opening, say twice a year. You'd all want to continue showing at galleries and so on, for the exposure, but if you each built up a mailing list and let everyone on it know about the kiln openings you could sell without giving anyone a cut. People might not want to trek out here just to see one potter's work; Elena was probably right about that. But I think they would come to see the work of a group of the finest potters around." He suddenly stopped. "Or am I way off base?"

It was Elena who answered. "No. No, you're not. I think you have an idea there."

"A sensational one!" Hap didn't hide his enthusiasm. "With the three of us living so close, it's a natural! Although I think we should bring in a couple more potters. Ones with contrasting styles. What about Sam Ducat? His work is raku," he added as an aside to Matt.

"Yeah," Sallie agreed excitedly. "And Jane . . . Oh, whatever her name is. You know, the one who lives toward Monroe. Does such fantastic things with salt glazes."

"Strasser," Elena contributed. "Jane Strasser. I'll bet she'd be interested. And what about . . ."

They were off and running. Matt just sat back and smiled as his suggestions became transformed into concrete plans. "Maybe late November," Hap said. "Perfect for the Christmas rush, and it'd give us all summer to build up a mailing list. Although we'd have to work our tails off to have a decent inventory. No September sigh of relief for us."

Elena met Matt's eyes. "I could live with that," she said to Hap, although she was still looking at Matt. "Listen, it's getting late and we'd better go. Why don't we talk to these other people? I'll call Jane, since I know her the best, and Sam's all yours. I think five is probably enough, don't you?"

Hap agreed, then turned to Matt. "I don't suppose you'd like to quit your job and become our full-time business manager, would you? Looks like we should have had one a long time ago."

Without thinking, Elena said wryly, "Matt's vice president of a bank, Hap. I don't think anything we can offer him will compete with that."

The amusement that had been in Matt's eyes was abruptly gone, replaced by a look she couldn't decipher. When he spoke to Hap, however, his tone was light. "Who knows, maybe I'll want to get out of the rat race someday and take you up on it. In the meantime, consider me a consultant."

Hap slapped him on the back. "Worth your weight in gold."

"Hey," Matt protested. "Better wait until after your sale before you congratulate me. What if it's a flop?"

"It won't be," Sallie said. "It makes too much sense."

Of course it made sense, Elena thought. Matt never said anything that didn't make sense. It was odd, really, that until tonight she hadn't faced how integral to his character that rational side of Matt was. It made her wonder if Matt was capable of setting that careful reason aside and going with his emotions instead. Even this delightful fling they were in the midst of made strange sense; she'd reasoned that out herself. Unfortunately, a permanent alliance was another matter. Why should he compromise on what he needed and wanted in a wife, merely because of some messy emotion?

And why was she thinking this way, anyway, when she was just as determined no future was possible for them? Come next Sunday, she told herself, she would have plenty of time to feel depressed. But right now she still had six days of happiness left and she refused to spoil them.

On that thought she scooted sideways on the car seat and laid her head against Matt's shoulder. His arm immediately came around her in a convulsive hug, and for just an instant she felt his lips move against her hair. Sexual tension was suddenly crackling in the air, and Elena badly wanted to feel his mouth against hers.

Matt echoed her feelings, his voice soft with intent. "It's a good thing the drive home is so short."

Elena's laugh was breathless. This was one subject, at least, on which she and Matt thought alike.

13

ELENA POKED her fork at the food on her plate. "I talked to Hap today," she said, her tone artificially bright. "I guess Sam Ducat is as excited by our idea as Jane was."

Matt nodded. "Good. I think this'll work out well for you."

"Yes, I'm sure it will."

Silence settled around them again as Elena tried to think of something else to say. Matt's contributions had been as sporadic and unspontaneous as her own, so even with the best will in the world on both sides, the conversation wasn't working.

It was Saturday night, their last dinner together. As the day had gone on, they'd both become quieter and more withdrawn. Elena was no longer certain what Matt was thinking behind the rigid mask his face had become, and she hoped in turn that he couldn't read her mind. He had guaranteed her nothing, made no promises for the future, and she had more pride than to let him see how miserable she was. She might feel like clutching his ankles and wailing, she thought unhappily, but she wouldn't. Instead, she would no doubt muster a brave smile and a casual wave when the time of his departure came. Then she could go bury her face in the pillow and sob.

Elena looked down now at the mostly uneaten goulash on her plate and decided they had sat there long enough. Dinner could safely be considered over. She picked up her plate and carried it over to the sink, scraping it in the garbage and then turning on the water to rinse it.

With her back to Matt and her eyes fixed unseeingly on the stream of running water, she asked abruptly, "When are you planning to leave?"

Matt didn't sound as though his mind was on his answer. "Before lunch, I suppose. I need to get settled at home, since I have to be at the bank early Monday."

That "at home" hurt. These past two weeks when he'd said home he had meant here. And she had begun to feel that this small log house she'd built was not only hers, but Matt's, as well. Still with her back to him, she said flatly, "I suppose you'll have a lot to catch up on."

"Yes."

At last she turned the water off and walked the few steps to the table to collect more dirty dishes. Matt was leaning back in his chair, his eyes watchful. For once he made no move to help her. She picked up dishes with perfectly steady hands, refusing to meet his gaze.

"Elena..." His voice had unexpectedly become husky. "We have to talk."

At last she looked at him, and her own eyes widened at the expression in his. She saw desperation and uncertainty that mirrored her own emotions.

"Yes," she said at last, on a choked whisper. "But not now. Tomorrow."

A muscle clenched in his jaw. "Tomorrow," he agreed.

Later, as they lay in bed together, their lovemaking had a different quality than it had ever had before. Outside there was a blustery wind that tumbled cumulus clouds across the night sky; every few minutes the waning moon made a brief appearance, so they were alternately bathed in translucent white light and shrouded in thick darkness. Under the warm covers of the bed, Matt and Elena touched and kissed with lingering sweetness. There was no urgency between them; it was as though they had all the time in the world. Or as if this was the only time they would have, so they were trying to make it last forever.

Elena ran her hands over Matt's body, imprinting on her memory the feel of him. With her lips she explored the lines of his face, and when their mouths met it was gently. There was no passionate duel, just a yielding on each part.

When they joined at last, their hips clung, reluctantly parting to come together again, and all the while their hands stroked and caressed. Matt's mouth never left Elena's and their breaths mingled.

For all that Elena would have liked this to last forever, a maelstrom of need soon caught her up and she lost control. The deliberate cadence Matt set was sweet agony for her, and she cried out his name as her hands moved frantically over the hard muscles of his shoulders and back. She was all feeling and Matt's body trembled under her hands as he, too, reached the apex they'd both wanted and yet tried to put off. Elena eventually drifted into sleep, her last fuzzy thought being that Matt's arms were wrapped securely around her. And he wasn't letting go.

As Matt cradled her in the dark, listening to her rhythmic breathing, his thoughts were troubled. These two weeks weren't ending as he'd hoped. He hadn't pressed her about the future during these days and nights because he had sensed that she wasn't ready, but now his back was to the wall. He couldn't go home tomorrow and call her casually for a date next Saturday. They had come too far for that. No, tomorrow he would ask her to marry him and hope that he was wrong about what her answer would be. On that thought his arms tightened ever so slightly around her, and he pressed a kiss to her temple.

When Elena awoke the next morning, it was to find herself alone in bed but for Pansy, who was curled in a tight ball at the foot. For just a moment she felt panic as she struggled upright to see that Matt's suitcase was still standing in the corner by the wardrobe. He wasn't gone. He'd just gotten up early, as he had on a few other mornings.

She found him in the kitchen with Leander and Marigold. They were meowing and circling his legs while he opened a can of cat food. He glanced up as Elena came in the room.

"Morning." His tone was normal but he wasn't smiling. "Sleep well?"

She headed unerringly for the coffeepot. "So-so."

"Try not to let Leander out, will you? He might not be around when I'm ready to leave."

"Okay," she agreed shortly, stung by the reminder of his imminent departure. "Have you had breakfast?"

"Toast." He tossed the empty can in the garbage and put the spoon in the sink. "Can I make you something? You look tired this morning."

Elena made a face. "Thanks for the compliment, but no, thanks. Toast will do for me, too."

Matt shrugged. "I'll go pack, then, and get that out of the way."

"Fine." She couldn't look at him. When he'd left the room, though, she slammed her mug down on the tile counter. Wiping up spilled coffee, she muttered under her breath, "Fine, terrific, wonderful!"

By the time he reappeared, however, she had regained much of her composure. She suspected that early morning grouchiness was a congenital defect, completely incurable. Although, she reflected, Matt had provided very effective therapy these past two weeks. There was nothing quite like smiling gray eyes and a gentle, erotically teasing touch to brighten her first waking thoughts.

She had just finished her two slices of toasted whole wheat bread covered with homemade raspberry jam and was draining her coffee cup when Matt appeared in the kitchen doorway. There was no sign of his suitcase.

"Are you ready to talk?" he asked evenly.

Elena's stomach plummeted, but she said with outward calm, "Sure. Why not?" She pushed her plate away and leaned her elbows on the table, watching as he pulled up a chair across from her.

There was silence for a moment while Matt studied Elena's face. He wasn't reassured when her eyes stayed stubbornly focused on the top button of his blue plaid sport shirt.

"I don't really know what's going on here, Elena," he said at last. "You've frozen up on me this past day or so."

Her gaze flew to his. "You call last night freezing up?"

He made an impatient gesture. "Not physically. You know that's not what I meant. Just in every other way."

Her gaze shied away again and she bit her lip, pushing herself away from the table and picking up her mug. Her voice was strained when she said, "I guess I have been a little . . . preoccupied. I'm sorry if it's bothered you."

Matt watched as she went over to the stove and poured another cup of coffee. "Like some?" she asked, holding up the pot.

He ignored her attempt at diversion. "Preoccupied with what?"

Elena carried the steaming mug back to the table, and he could almost see the wheels turning in her mind as she debated how honest to be with him. "I guess," she said finally, "I've been wondering if this wasn't a mistake."

"My being here?"

She nodded.

There was another long pause before Matt said, "I've enjoyed every minute of it, Elena."

Her eyes unwillingly met his again. "I have, too," she admitted. "I'm going to miss you."

"You don't have to, you know," he said quietly. "I'd like you to marry me."

In one way Elena had expected this, even armed herself against it. Still, her pulse skyrocketed and for one delirious minute she allowed herself to dream. But then common sense took over; they weren't—couldn't be—dreaming the same dream. In hers the future unfolded as a continuation of the past two weeks, unhurried, untouched by the outside world. But in Matt's dreams, this life would be left behind; she would become an adjunct to the life he'd always been living. Maybe they were both basically selfish, she thought, each wanting to keep a life they were satisfied with, neither wanting to give way.

"These two weeks have been...good," she said softly. "I'll admit that. But I don't think they've changed any of our basic differences."

He sighed. "It would have been unrealistic to expect that they would. I can't change what I am. I know you'd like me to say I want to give up my job, move in with you, let the world go on its merry way without me. Well, I can't do that. I'd be miserable. I'm good at what I do, and it suits me. I can't give that up. And why should I have to?"

"I've never suggested you should," Elena said truthfully. She'd only dreamed it.

Matt reached his hand across the table to her, and his voice was warmly persuasive. "Elena, we both knew this would be fun, but we also knew it couldn't go on forever. Now it's time to get back to the real world." He was opening his mouth to say more when she interrupted in sudden outrage.

"What makes you think this isn't real?"

Matt knew he'd blundered, but he had gone too far to pull back now. "Your life here is a fairy tale," he said bluntly. "Even you must realize it's no more than a pleasant interlude. You supposedly run a business, but you don't bother to do it efficiently. You sabotage yourself before you can make a profit. That doesn't tell me that you're taking it very seriously. In fact, nothing you do is done wholeheartedly. You garden, but not on a scale to really feed yourself. You pot, but not full-time. You live the 'simple life,' but you have electricity, washing machine, Rototiller. All the comforts of modern society. Do you know what I think, Elena?"

"I can guess," she said, her chin held proudly high but her eyes dark with undisguised pain.

Matt wanted to stop and take her in his arms, beg her to agree to share his life, but his core of anger drove him on. The cabin and the land, the garden and even the animals, Elena had chosen them over him.

"I think you're rebelling against your parents," he said. "You're acting out a life-style as much in opposition to theirs as you can manage, but you're not doing it from any deep ideology. No, you just want to make them mad. Well, you're old enough now to see your own motivation and put it behind you. You and I aren't that different, not as different as you're determined to think."

Answering anger had kindled in her eyes as he spoke, and it was those sparks that brought him abruptly to his senses and to an awareness of what a fool he'd been. Had he even meant what he'd said?

"Elena." He had to try again. His tone was altered as he fumbled for the right words. "I'm not your father all over again. And I'm not that fiancé you were smart enough to get rid off. I don't expect the same things from you that he did. That's what you're afraid of, isn't it? It's true you might have to make outward compromises. Obviously we couldn't live here, for example. But I don't expect . . ."

Elena pushed back from the table, cutting him off. "It's all what *you* expect! What about what I expect? But you've never even thought about it, have you? No, you've labeled me as immature because I've chosen to live differently from you. But I'm sure," she said with exaggerated sweetness, "you think that with your firm guidance, I'll soon change. After all, I'm attractive and reasonably intelligent. I should make a model wife, with a little work on your part, of course." She dropped the pose and said bitterly, "Was I supposed to be impressed by your little speech? Did you think I'd blush and fall into your arms?"

Matt didn't move, even though she was standing now and he had to tilt his head back to see her. He fought for calm. "Elena, let's be reasonable."

It was like waving a red flag in front of a bull. "Reasonable!" she snapped. "Don't insult me, Matt."

"I had no such intention."

His outward composure, bought with an effort she didn't see, infuriated Elena still further. "Of course not!"

she exclaimed rashly. "An insult might imply some emotion! And that's not your style, is it?"

"If you can say that, you don't know me very well," he said harshly.

Elena voluntarily fell back a pace from the dangerous storm brewing in his eyes, but she held her head high and refused to be intimidated. He'd said hurtful things to her, and she was going to say them back. "It's the truth, whether you know it or not!" she flung at him. "Compared to us mere mortals, you think like a computer. Your brain is always clicking away, no matter what, analyzing the facts, coming to conclusions. And it's those conclusions that rule you, isn't it? I'll bet you've never in your life done something just because your heart told you it was right! Not if your brain said it was foolish! Because emotions have to be kept firmly under control, don't they?"

Matt's mouth twisted. "I haven't succeeded very well where you're concerned, have I?"

His words thundering in her ears, Elena stared at him. At last she swallowed. "What . . . what do you mean?" she faltered.

"I love you," he said. The words dropped like chunks of ice. He was looking at her with something very near dislike. "There, is that what you needed to hear? Do the words sweeten the pot? Because I've damned well shown you how I feel! And I always thought actions were supposed to speak louder than words."

Tiredness mixed with despair had settled into Matt's very bones. Maybe Elena was right. Maybe she'd been right about him all along. *Had* he assumed he could reshape her, that she'd put aside those parts of her life that were an inconvenience to him the moment he asked? "Tell me where I went wrong, Elena," he said in a low voice. "What is it you need from me?"

She backed up to her chair and sat down again, showing a weariness that matched his. "I don't know," she said. "Maybe I needed you to be someone different than you are. Someone who could open up and share, turn to me for comfort. And you'll never be able to, will you?" Her eyes searched his rigid face. "But it's more than that. I need you to see me as a person whose values and priorities and dreams have as much validity as yours. I need you to respect me. But you don't. You've told me that just now. If I were truly grown-up, I'd be just like you, isn't that what you were saying?"

For the first time a dark flush rose in Matt's cheeks. Before he could open his mouth to protest, however, she continued.

"Who knows, maybe I don't see you any more accurately than you see me. After all—" she gave a faint, wry smile "—I'd have liked to change you, too. I wanted to see you open up to me, throw your heart over the windmill. I've been telling myself what separated us were physical things: I don't want to be a banker's wife, to give up my potting or my freedom to be and say what suits me. But those are just externals. What's important is the way you think, and the way I think. And how much we value each other's opinions. I guess right now that's not very much, is it?"

"Then there's nothing more to say, is there?"

Elena pressed her lips together to hold back the tears and shook her head. Her fingernails were biting into her palms, but she was only peripherally aware of the pain, so consumed was she by the deeper agony that twisted in her chest.

Matt stood up, the movement slow and lacking in his usual easy grace. He walked stiffly to the door, as though his joints hurt. "I'll have to find Leander."

She nodded. "I'll get your carrier."

It was wonderful how they could be polite to the bitter end, she thought unhappily. Although what was the alternative? They weren't angry, so they couldn't scream. The despair they both felt could only be expressed in tears, and she doubted that Matt ever cried. She had too much pride to do it in front of him, under the circumstances.

When he reappeared, she held the carrier out while he stuffed in the protesting cat. "Goodbye, Leander," she whispered, and was answered with a mournful howl.

She even walked out to the car with Matt, as she would have done with any departing visitor, and watched while he deposited his suitcase in the trunk and the cat carrier on the front seat. He opened his own door before turning to look at her one last time.

Elena nearly gasped at what she saw in his eyes. The shutters were gone. Deliberately, it seemed, he was letting her see his pain, which in this shattering instant hurt her more than did her own.

"I do love you," he said quietly.

She couldn't have responded to save her life.

"Do you know," he added, "you've never said the same to me."

HER ENTIRE LIFE happened in cycles, thought Elena wretchedly. She was beginning to feel that it was her fate to stand for eternity here in the silent clearing, straining her ears for the last sounds of his car. Only each time seemed more painful than the last.

She turned and walked into the house, her movements as stiff as Matt's had been. When Dahlia bumped her leg, she stroked the dog's head mechanically, and when she got upstairs she was glad that none of the cats occupied the bed. She just wanted to be alone. Right now, the blind love her animals could give her was no solace; it was more of an intrusion.

She would have liked to cry, but tears wouldn't come. So she lay on her side on the bed, staring dry-eyed and unseeing toward the bright windows, not even noticing the change of light as morning drew into afternoon.

It was Jamaal nudging her with his wet nose that roused her at last. He was hungry, and if he was the others must be. For that matter, she realized with surprise, she was, too. A glance at the clock told her it was midafternoon. Two pieces of toast weren't enough to hold her for an entire day, but it seemed unromantic to eat. A heroine in a novel would have fasted, wasting away into fragile nothingness. But then, when it came right down to it, what was romantic about being miserable? And that's what she was: achingly, heart-wrenchingly miserable.

She stayed that way. She went through the motions of living in the days that followed, but her mind remained mired in thoughts of Matt. At night she dreamed about him, in the morning she ached for him, during the day she wondered about him. What was he doing right this minute? Was he thinking of her? Did he miss her? And, most important of all, did it have to end this way? Was there any chance she'd been wrong?

His accusation that her entire way of life was nothing more than a rebellion against her parents had cut deeply. Now she forced herself to examine it with clear eyes. As she thought, she worked, tying up peas. She pounded stakes into the ground, then strung twine between them, at last wrapping the thin, leafy vines around the line. It was a task that should have been done days before.

Maybe, Elena admitted to herself, in an uncomfortable bout of honesty, she *had* been secretly pleased at her father's reaction when she first moved here. Of course, it wasn't a conscious pleasure. She had told herself then, a little self-righteously, that it was too bad if her parents were hurt by her decision, but that it was their own fault. After all, she was rejecting their lifestyle and values for good reason. Anyway, they would come to accept her as she was.

They had, but it had taken years. And they'd never become actually proud of her. What her existence lacked, from their point of view, was success. In a way, it was the same thing to which Matt had objected. She didn't do anything quite well enough that they could brag to their friends about it. Matt had put it differently. He'd said she didn't put her whole heart into anything.

Elena was relentless in examining her motives, but she couldn't find even a twinge of that postadolescent rebellion. Matt was wrong. She loved her parents, enjoyed seeing them once a year, but she no longer needed their approval or reveled in their disapproval. If it was true that her feelings toward them had played a role in her decision to change her life-style, they had been long since forgotten. She had found a deep inner satisfaction with her life here and had stayed with it because it made her happy, and for no other reason.

Where her feelings toward her parents did matter, she realized with an unpleasant twinge of surprise, was when it came to her perception of Matt. From the moment she'd met him she'd seen him through a filter of leftover anger felt for both her father and the businessmen she'd encountered during her brief financial career. Because Matt was a banker, a man who dealt in dollars and power, who wore that same air of confidence, she had decided he was like them. Right or wrong, she had never lost that certainty.

But Matt wasn't the same man Jeff had been, Elena thought with a curious thrill of pride. Matt certainly wouldn't need a prop, as Jeff obviously had. If anything, Matt went too far the other way, refusing to acknowledge and therefore share what might be weakening emotions.

But maybe he could learn. She remembered that devastating glimpse into his inner pain just before he'd left, a glimpse he had freely given her. Anyway, as he had pointed out, she hadn't been any freer with her emotions than he had been. And that wasn't like her. The trouble was, she had been positive from the very beginning that a long-term relationship with Matt wouldn't work, and from then on she might as well have been wearing blinders. She had never given him an honest chance. And he had been more than patient with her.

Elena dropped her gardening tools where they fell and wandered into the house. After pouring herself a glass of iced tea, she sat out on the front steps in the shade. She'd done some terrific reasoning, she thought wryly, but where did it lead her? Matt wasn't going to come knocking on her door again to tell her he would like to discuss the matter further. Nor could she stroll into his office at the bank to ask casually, "By the way, what *do* you want in a wife?"

"Elena Simpson," she said aloud, "you blew it but good!"

It took three more increasingly lonely days before Elena knew she was going to have to see Matt and admit how wrong she had been. The thought was not palatable. He would have every reason in the world to laugh in her face. Or to sit there behind that wide oak desk and listen to her faltering apologies before ushering her out.

Well, she wouldn't be any worse off if that did happen than she was now, and at the moment she was wretched down to her very bones. She wasn't sleeping well at night, she was neglecting her animals, her potting, her friends. She *needed* Matt.

It was almost laughable to think how unwilling she had been to compromise, all the while accusing Matt of just that. Somehow she'd come to invest her log cabin, her garden, her work, with an importance they didn't have. She'd believed that if Matt asked her to give any of them up, he would be asking her to surrender a part of herself. But was she so insecure as a person that she would lose her bearings simply because her surroundings changed? She didn't think so.

Of course there *were* differences between them that counted. What if he told her he wanted to move on to a high-powered bank in New York City? What if he didn't think he could live with her casual housekeeping, her refusal to tailor her conversation to the company? She could think of a million small problems that might mushroom into large ones.

On Sunday when Elena at last swallowed her pride and decided to at least call Matt, she discovered he had an unlisted phone number. That meant she would have to go into the bank, and she would have to wait until tomorrow.

The day passed with agonizing slowness. Elena debated with herself whether she should make an appointment to see him. She pictured driving into town only to find him too busy to fit her in. That would be more than disappointing; it would be humiliating. On the other hand, she thought it might be better just to take him by surprise. At least then she would have the satisfaction of seeing his face—a small consolation if he refused to listen or was simply no longer interested.

By Monday she was a quivering mass of uncertainties. Maybe he *was* the man she had originally thought him to be. Maybe all her careful reasoning this last week had been warped by the fact that she missed him, that she wanted to have been wrong about him. If that was so, she was making a big mistake.

She sighed as she stood up and dumped her cold toast in the garbage. This was something she had to do.

An hour later she was ready to go, although not feeling any braver. She'd changed from her jeans to a pair of khaki poplin slacks and a cotton blouse with cap sleeves and a print of big splashy peach and rust flowers. Her thick hair was wound into a silky knot at the back of her head. When she looked at herself in the mirror, she saw an attractive, poised young woman looking back at her. There was no sign of the mingled terror and hope churning inside on her face.

Forty minutes later she was walking into the bank. Even before the door began to swing shut behind her, she was glancing apprehensively around. But business was being conducted as usual. The loan officers were busy at their desks, none of the tellers even glanced up, and of the customers waiting in line only a small girl holding her mother's hand turned to eye her.

Elena took a deep breath and walked toward Matt's office. The light was on, but from this angle she couldn't see whether he was inside or not. She pinned a smile on her face for the moment when his secretary looked up, but as she paused in front of the desk, her gaze went beyond. Matt *was* there.

Unfortunately, he wasn't alone. An elderly man sat across from him. There were papers strewed on the desk in front of Matt, and pen in hand, he was listening with an expression of bland courtesy. Elena recognized that look from her own initial interview with him.

She was so transfixed by the sight of him that it took her a moment to realize his secretary had spoken. She could feel warmth in her cheeks and she shifted her gaze to the woman's face.

"I'm sorry," she said. "I'm afraid my mind was wandering." To where, she feared, was all too obvious.

The secretary's smile was kind and a little amused. "Don't apologize. You're Miss Simpson, aren't you? I'm afraid Mr. Terrell has a client with him at the moment, but if you don't mind waiting, I'm sure he'll want to see you as soon as he's free."

Elena wasn't so sure, but she returned the woman's smile and thanked her.

Before taking one of the chairs that stood just outside his office she glanced in again, her eyes drawn there despite her attempt at appearing casual. This time her gaze met Matt's. He froze, pen poised to write, his incredulity plain. They stared at each other through the wall of glass for what seemed an eternity until Matt finally blinked and shook his head slightly, as though trying to determine if she was a figment of his imagination. Elena swallowed hard and dropped into the armchair she'd bumped into.

The door to his magical sanctum didn't burst open, as it would have if she had been the one on the other side of it. It didn't open for ten long minutes. Elena watched every one of those minutes pass on the bank clock, hearing the nearly imperceptible click as the hand moved forward yet again. She twisted her fingers in her lap, smiled occasionally at the secretary, and imagined this was what it would be like waiting for her turn at the guillotine.

If only she knew what Matt was thinking. His expression had told her nothing, except that he was surprised. Not that she had been foolish enough to expect joy, but she had hoped to read *some* emotion on his face. She clung to the memory of the last time she'd seen him, and the look in his eyes when he'd said he loved her. However hurt he had been by her rejection, love didn't die in a week. There had to be some hope.

When the door beside her at last swung open, her pulse accelerated with a frantic leap. Taking a deep breath to calm herself, she rose slowly to her feet. Matt didn't look at her as he came out; Elena suspected he had deliberately chosen to stand with his back to her as he exchanged courtesies with the older man.

They at last shook hands, and as his client walked away Matt turned to face Elena. His expression was carefully controlled. "Come in, Elena," he said quietly.

She numbly preceded him into the office, noting with despair that he didn't even bother to shut the door. Perhaps that was a less than subtle hint that he didn't want to hear what she had to say.

Elena stopped in the middle of the carpeted floor. "Matt . . ."

"I don't want to talk here." He circled the desk and leaned over to pick up his briefcase. She watched with disbelief as he began shoveling papers into it. After a minute he snapped it shut. "All right, let's go."

"Go where?" she questioned weakly.

His answer wasn't very illuminating. "I have something I want to show you. I was going to give you a call."

"You do?" she repeated dumbly. What on earth was going on here? Maybe it was just an excuse to get her out of the bank, she thought, but that didn't make sense, either. She wouldn't have argued if he had suggested they talk in the car. He didn't need to employ subterfuge.

When Matt gestured toward the door, Elena shrugged and went. If this once he wanted her to follow him with blind faith, she would oblige. She owed him that much.

He paused beside his secretary's desk. "I'll be out for a few hours," he informed her. "Until after lunch, at least."

A moment later Elena was sitting stiffly against the black leather upholstery as Matt steered the Mercedes out of the lot. She studied his set profile.

"Matt," she began tentatively, "I've done a lot of thinking since last Sunday."

He shook his head. "Let's talk after we get there. What I want to show you is...well, ammunition for my cause. So if you don't mind . . ."

Elena's heart began to race. Ammunition? If only he weren't being so mysterious, she thought with frustration. She didn't feel very patient right now.

She *was* intrigued, though, and more hopeful than she had been in a long while. The least she could do was humor him, Elena thought. With a sigh she leaned back in her seat and turned from Matt's unrevealing profile to watch the passing scenery.

15

ELENA WAS soon even more puzzled about their destination. Matt drove out of town toward Everett, but in just a few miles angled off the old highway onto a narrow country road. They jogged several more times, onto increasingly less traveled roads. When Matt finally slowed to make the turn through an open gate onto a narrow, two-track lane, Elena sat forward eagerly. The woods bordering the lane on one side were not as dense as hers and were comprised mostly of alders and maples. The other side was pasture fenced by rusting barbed wire, the grass overgrown. The lane was rising slightly and ahead she could see a house—a large, two-story white clapboard with a graceful, wraparound porch and a neat but weathered barn.

Matt pulled the Mercedes to a stop beside the barn and turned off the ignition. Still he remained silent, offering no explanation. After a minute Elena opened the car door and climbed out, looking around with a pang of envy.

From the leaded glass windows inset on each side of the front door to the glimpse she had through the large front windows of oak woodwork and the foot of a curved stair rail with a newel post, the house was perfect—a beautiful country Victorian. It must have five bedrooms, she thought, narrowing her eyes against the sun. And an enormous kitchen. Several huge lilac bushes in glorious purple bloom crowded the porch and scented the air with sweetness. To provide the crowning touch, there was even a small duck pond in the pasture, complete with ducks.

The house appeared freshly painted, white but for the black that trimmed the windows and accentuated the gingerbread along the eaves and porch. It was obviously empty, however. The windows were curtainless, and the grounds had an unmistakable air of neglect. So why had Matt brought her here? She turned to face him with renewed determination as he began to walk toward her. He had left his suit jacket in the car and was already tugging impatiently at his tie as he walked.

Matt had been watching Elena's changing expressions with carefully concealed anxiety from the moment he had helped her into the car. He was tempted now to throw this whole crazy idea out; just because she was willing to talk again didn't mean she'd changed her mind. And what could he say that would mean anything to her? No, this was best. He would give the house a chance to speak for him, to show her how he envisioned their life together.

Pausing in front of her, he asked casually, as though this were an everyday situation, "So what do you think?"

She blinked in surprise. "You mean of the house?" At his nod she shrugged helplessly. "It's charming, of course. Whose is it?"

Matt made a pretense of glancing around, although he watched her out of the corner of his eye. "It's for sale."

Elena had to close her eyes to block the sudden wave of desire that swept over her. Desire for Matt, and for the house with all it represented. She could so easily imagine the two of them lazing on that porch swing, holding hands, the scent of baking bread drifting from the kitchen and mingling with that of the lilacs. There would be horses grazing peacefully in the pasture and maybe, someday, the sound of children laughing as they played on the broad lawn. For all it's charm, she thought wistfully, this house needed something; it seemed to cry out for a family.

The dawning joy that tingled along her nerves brought a warning in its wake. It was difficult to imagine that after Elena had refused to marry him, Matt had spent the week house-hunting anyway.

"That really doesn't answer my question," she finally said.

Matt gave her an unexpectedly beguiling smile. "Why don't we look around inside? I have the key."

Elena didn't move. "Why don't you tell me what this is all about first?"

"About?" He managed to look surprised. "Oh, I'm thinking of buying this place. As an investment."

She gulped. "You are?"

"Of course, I haven't entirely made up my mind," he continued blandly. "That's why I'd like to know what you think. I have a great deal of respect for your opinion, you know."

The reference was impossible to mistake, and Elena raised her eyebrows. "Have I ever doubted that?" she murmured.

Matt gave a snort of laughter before gesturing toward the house. "Shall we?"

She almost groaned with frustration. Was he torturing her deliberately? He had referred to what he wanted to show her as ammunition, and she could think of only one meaning to that. But she didn't dare let herself believe Matt had this house in mind because he shared her vision.

As she considered Matt's motivation Elena's feet slowly took her up the shallow front steps. The porch was wider than it had looked from the lawn, more like an open-air room with railings broad enough to sit on. The swing, freshly painted to match the house, hung from chains; she had to restrain herself from trying it out.

"Nice," Matt said appreciatively. He was surveying the sweep of lawn and pasture that was visible from where they stood. "I like the pond, don't you?"

Whatever the nature of Matt's game, her participation was obviously required. "Yes," she agreed. "Let's go in."

He inserted the large key in the old-fashioned keyhole, then stepped aside with exaggerated courtesy for her to enter before him. Elena passed him with scant attention to the beauty of the oak door or even those leaded glass windows she had admired from the car.

Once inside, however, she stopped dead in the middle of the floor. If she had admired the house from outside, even coveted it, now she had fallen in love. The entry hall was wide and gracious, the floor oak parquet. The staircase that led to the upper floor was lovely; she longed to run her hand along its smooth, curved railing. Through a door with carved molding, she could see the living room, or what would have been called the parlor when this house had been built around the turn of the century.

"How did you find this place?" she asked in hushed tones.

He was watching her reaction with a strangely intent gaze. "I knew the people who used to live here. I had business dealings with them and admired the house then. Just by chance I heard it was up for sale."

Elena squeezed the words out. "Are you thinking of living here?"

Matt shrugged, his gaze not leaving her face. "Maybe. Although it's a little large for one person."

Cat and mouse, she thought, on a surge of glorious hope. He could be hinting at only one thing. "Yes, it is." She looked innocently at him. "It would be perfect for children, don't you think?"

His mouth curved. "There are certainly enough bedrooms."

"Mmm." She stepped past him into the living room. Without furniture it had a ghostly air, or a sense of waiting, like a ballroom just before the beautifully gowned ladies sweep in on their escort's gallant arms.

Elena shook off the fanciful thought and walked briskly across the polished parquet floor and through the arched opening into the next room, which to her astonishment and pleasure turned out to be a library.

"Oh, Matt!" she breathed, turning slowly on her heels to take in the built-in oak shelves, some of which had glass doors. "I've always wanted a house with a library!"

His smile was satisfied, even smug, and told Elena more clearly than words how much her reaction meant to him. She felt so full of joy she wanted to twirl on her toes like a ballerina, and yet she was conscious of sadness, as well. Had she humbled Matt so much that he thought he had to bribe her with the perfect house?

She turned jerkily away from him. "Let's look at the kitchen."

Kitchens most often showed the era of a house, but this one had been remodeled with love and respect. The old cupboards had been left, although the Italian tile that now topped the counters couldn't have been original, the dishwasher and porcelain sink certainly weren't. Small paned windows let in a wash of light, and Elena could imagine the round oak table that would complete the room.

"Oh, damn," she whispered, then glanced at Matt, her lips compressed. She was rapidly reaching her limit. If he didn't say something meaningful soon, preferably "I love you," she might turn into a gibbering idiot. Imagining how Matt would react if she threw back her head and gave a blood-curdling scream promptly restored her humor. The house obviously symbolized something to him. It was more than a pleasant place for them to live, and if he wanted her to see every nook and cranny before they talked, then so be it.

The next stop on their tour was a glassed-in back porch. Bright, roomy and heated, it would make a perfect studio for a potter.

Matt stood in the middle, his hands shoved casually in the pockets of his slacks. He glanced around as though seeing the room for the first time.

"Looks like your sun porch, doesn't it? Bigger, though." His eyes had a mischievous glint as they met hers. "There'd even be room for your kiln." He smiled and then suddenly switched tacks. "But I haven't quite decided what to do with it. What do you think? Maybe an extra sitting room? With overstuffed chairs, lots of plants, old-fashioned wallpaper?"

Elena scarcely heard him, so busy was she arranging in her mind where her kiln and wheel and shelves should go. "Lovely," she agreed absently.

Matt's smile was slow and almost sensuous. "Why do I get the feeling you didn't even hear my last suggestion?"

A delicious shiver ran down Elena's spine and curled her toes, and she had to take a deep breath and look away. Still, she had enough self-control to shrug with an attempt at nonchalance. "I guess studios interest me more than sitting rooms. After all, I'm not an interior decorator."

His mouth quirked. "Doesn't the house make you want to dabble?"

She had to answer truthfully. "No. It's perfect the way it is."

His smile deepened again, and Elena decided it was time to beat a strategic retreat.

Matt followed as she led the way up the graceful staircase to the second floor and flung open the first door in the hall. Elena found herself in a large bedroom, and despite her flustered awareness of Matt at her heels, her breath caught at its appeal. The woodwork in here was white, and the large windows had the small panes she loved in her own house. The wallpaper was also white with a delicate pattern of blue and green and peach butterflies; it was light and airy and restful, and suited the house perfectly.

Matt's voice came suddenly from behind her, deep and a little rough. "I thought this should be the master bedroom." He paused and added, "Our bedroom."

Elena's eyes widened as his words reverberated in her mind, sending ripples of sheer happiness from her suddenly tight chest to every nerve in her body. Slowly she turned to face Matt, knowing with unshakable certainty what she would see on his face, "Our?" she repeated, her voice quivering ever so slightly.

Her knees nearly buckled at the heart-stopping tenderness and desire in his eyes. But it was the uncertainty that touched her most.

"I'd like to buy the house for us," he said gruffly. "If you think you could be happy here."

"Happy?" Tears battled Elena's dawning smile. "Oh, Matt. You must know I love it." Impulsively she held out her hands to him. "But not nearly as much as I love you."

Matt was more shaken by those three small words than he'd ever expected to be. "Do you mean that?"

"Of course I do." she whispered. "Why do you think I came to see you today?"

"I hoped." Even to his own ears his voice was ragged. "But I couldn't be sure."

"Matt..." Elena looked unaccustomedly hesitant. "Did you think I wouldn't have you without the house? Is that why we're here?"

"No." He smiled crookedly. "I know you better than that. I just thought it might show you how I feel, prove that I don't expect you to change. There's room for a studio, children... whatever you want." He'd never been more sincere, or more desperate for her acceptance. "My being a banker won't have to interfere. I need to entertain once in a while or go to the odd affair, but if you'd give me those rare times the rest of our life can be the way you want it. I promise."

The swell of happiness that washed over Elena was closely followed by shame. "No, Matt," she said quietly. His face tightened and she hurried on, "Not the way I want it. We'll make our life the way *we* want it. I'm not a child who always has to have her way, even if I've been acting like one."

He stiffened. "Do you mean...?'

"I'll marry you," she said, "if you really still want me."

"Want you?" His eyes were molten silver. "What do you think?"

Elena had to blink back a mist of tears. "I think I'm lucky you're a patient man."

"Patient?" Matt echoed again. He took one long stride and swept her into his arms, his strong fingers tilting her face up to his. "I may be many things, but patient isn't one of them." His mouth came down on hers with a passionate intensity that proved his words.

Elena wound her arms tightly around his neck and kissed him with equal fervency, not caring that he was crushing her against him so hard she could barely breathe. At this moment, she thought dazedly, nothing matters but Matt, not even air.

When at last Matt pulled back just a little, his grip didn't loosen and his eyes glowed with a light that sent a shiver down Elena's spine. "This room is missing only one thing," he said huskily. "A bed. I think we'd better remedy that soon."

"Very soon," she agreed softly, and then his lips were on hers again, not as forcefully this time, but with tender sensuality.

Elena reveled in this kiss. The taste of Matt's mouth, the supple texture of his big hands caressing her, the feel of his shoulder muscles under her touch. It seemed that the way they related physically symbolized all the rest. Matt was a man who could blend laughter with passion, who was always sensitive to what pleased her and who tempered his strength with gentleness. Deep down she had always known that, even while she had been telling herself how closed and rigid he was.

A good fifteen minutes later they made their way down to the porch. They sat in the swing, alternating talking with kissing.

Elena told Matt some of what she had thought this past week. "There's one thing I want you to know," she said firmly, pushing back from him enough to be able to see his face. "I *am* serious about my potting, Matt. It's not a game for me at all. I've been making a living at it for several years." When he opened his mouth to interrupt, she pressed her finger to his lips to stop the words. "I know, I could make more money. But then, so could you. You decided not to take an offer from one of the big Wall Street banks because you didn't want to live in New York. I don't want to work any harder because I want time for other things. What's the difference?"

"Not much," he agreed. "But that isn't what I was going to say at all. I've done a lot of thinking, too, you know. And I realized that particular accusation of mine was especially ironic, because one of the qualities about you that attracts me the most is your air of serenity, of inner quiet. I suspect you have that for the very reason I criticized: because you aren't ambitious, always driving yourself. You let yourself be contented with the small moments. And I wouldn't want you to be any other way. In fact—" his smile was rueful "—I hope you'll work on me."

She curled contentedly back into the circle of his arm. "I can live with your drive," she assured him. "Unless you neglect me, of course. Or our children. You wouldn't do that, would you?"

"Never," he vowed with heart-stopping sincerity.

He pressed a butterfly kiss on her temple, then moved his lips down the soft line of her cheek. His hand lazily cupped one breast, and he took her earlobe gently between his teeth. After a moment he gave it a sharp nip and released it. "Damn it, Elena," he complained. "Here we are in our own house, and there's no place to make love. That's a ridiculous state of affairs, isn't it?"

Her eyes only half-open, Elena gave the matter serious thought. "There's always the grass," she suggested. "Why don't we go down by the duck pond?"

She could feel his smile against the top of her head. "That's what I like about you," he said on a breath of laughter. "You're creative. So what are we waiting for?"

They were strolling across the pasture when Matt asked unexpectedly, "What is it you were afraid of with me, Elena? Why did you keep running? I still don't really understand."

She stopped and looked straight at him. "Does it really matter now?"

There was a moment of silence, and then he said with faint surprise, "No. I guess it doesn't. I only wish I could take back some of those things I said just to hurt you. I was angry Sunday, and more than a little frustrated that you hadn't fallen right into my arms the way you were supposed to." He added wryly, "Arrogant of me, wasn't it?"

Her answering smile was brimming with love. "But then, excessive humility has never been one of your faults, has it?"

"Or pandering to a man's ego one of yours."

Filled with dizzying happiness, Elena chuckled and slipped her arms around Matt's neck. "I pander to other things much better," she murmured in a deliberately sexy voice.

Matt's hands slid down to her waist, and he pulled her intimately against him. "Are you trying to distract me?"

Her brows raised in mock surprise. "From what?"

"Since you put it that way..."

They dropped right where they stood, on the soft grass beside the small pond. Ducks bobbed in the sun-lit green water without concern for their presence, sending minute ripples to lap the shore.

Matt laid her back on the grass and leaned over her, propped on his elbows and forearms. The sun was just behind his head.

Elena reached up and stroked his lean cheek. "I love you, Matt." Her heart was in her voice.

"I love you, too, Elena. More than you can imagine."

"Oh, I can imagine," she whispered. "I can feel it when you touch me, Matt."

His lips curved into a ghost of a smile. "Then I'll give you a practical demonstration, shall I?"

His mouth came down on hers with all the hunger of that missing week. As Elena melted in Matt's embrace, twining her arms about his neck and parting her lips under the insistent pressure of his, she knew there would be more than enough time to make up for those lost days.

Coming Next Month
From JoAnn Ross!!!

Tempting Fate

Professor Donovan Kincaid didn't believe in fate, but Brooke Stirling's return to Smiley College *had* to be more than coincidence. Twelve years earlier they'd been fellow students—and lovers—until he'd broken Brooke's heart. Now Donovan was determined to resurrect the love and passion they'd once shared. Brooke was equally determined to resist....

#153 *Tempting Fate* is the final book in the "Lucky Penny" trilogy by bestselling author JoAnn Ross. The magic penny first brought good fortune and romance in #126 *Magic in the Night*, followed by #137 *Playing for Keeps*. Look for *Tempting Fate* in May 1987!

LUCK-1-BPA

What the press says about Harlequin romance fiction…

"When it comes to romantic novels…
Harlequin is the indisputable king."
— *New York Times*

"…always with an upbeat, happy ending."
— *San Francisco Chronicle*

"Women have come to trust these
stories about contemporary people,
set in exciting foreign places."
— *Best Sellers*, New York

"The most popular reading matter of
American women today."
— *Detroit News*

"…a work of art."
— *Globe & Mail*, Toronto

**For the millions who can't read
Give the Gift of Literacy**

One out of five adults in North America
cannot read or write well enough
to fill out a job application
or understand the directions on a bottle of medicine.

**You can change all this by joining the fight
against illiteracy.**

For more information write to:
Contact, Box 81826, Lincoln, Neb. 68501
In the United States, call toll free: 800-228-3225

**The only degree you need
is a degree of caring**

LIT—A—1

Harlequin Temptation

COMING NEXT MONTH

#153 TEMPTING FATE JoAnn Ross

Donovan Kincaid didn't believe in fate—but Brooke Stirling's sudden reappearance in his life made him think again. He wasn't about to let her escape a second time....

#154 THE ROAD HOME Christine Rimmer

Rachel Davis had every intention of keeping her past and present quite separate. But Kane Walker was determined to bring the two together—with himself firmly in her future.

#155 CUPID'S CAPER
Vicki Lewis Thompson

A serious student of handwriting analysis, Cassie Larue was intrigued by Andrew Bennett's penmanship. And passionately interested in his downstrokes....

#156 THE MARRYING KIND
Rosalind Carson

Kerry Ryan was the kind of man who made a woman's toes curl when he kissed her. The problem was, he wasn't at all the marrying kind...and Nora Courtney was.

ATTRACTIVE, SPACE SAVING BOOK RACK

Display your most prized novels on this handsome and sturdy book rack. The hand-rubbed walnut finish will blend into your library decor with quiet elegance, providing a practical organizer for your favorite hard-or soft-covered books.

Only $9.95

Approximately 16" x 8" when assembled

Assembles in seconds!

To order, rush your name, address and zip code, along with a check or money order for $10.70* ($9.95 plus 75¢ postage and handling) payable to *Harlequin Reader Service*:

Harlequin Reader Service
Book Rack Offer
901 Fuhrmann Blvd.
P.O. Box 1325
Buffalo, NY 14269-1325

Offer not available in Canada.

*New York residents add appropriate sales tax.

BKR-1R